SAM CRESCENT & STACEY ESPINO

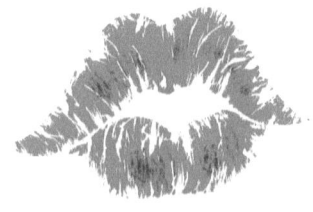

EVERNIGHT PUBLISHING ®

www.evernightpublishing.com

CHARMING ASSHOLE

Copyright© 2017

Sam Crescent & Stacey Espino

Editor: Karyn White

Cover Artist: Jay Aheer

ISBN: 978-1-77339-347-6

ALL RIGHTS RESERVED

SAM CRESCENT & STACEY ESPINO

CHARMING ASSHOLE

Killer of Kings, 3

Sam Crescent & Stacey Espino

Copyright © 2017

Chapter One

"Where the fuck are you?" Boss asked.

Killian sighed and was tempted to hang up, but Boss was his paycheck, so he didn't like to be rude. "I told you I needed a fucking break, and I'm not coming back in to do a job, or stop your ass from getting killed."

When Boss had taken Scarlett, who happened to be Bain's woman, it had gone against every single moral code that Killian possessed. Bain worked for Boss at Killer of Kings, where Killian also worked. It was an organization that arranged hitmen for hire. If you wanted someone taken out, and could pay the large fee, that person would be dead within the stated deadline.

Bain had gone against Boss's orders, and then the fucker had shot him, causing Boss to take revenge. That had resulted in Scarlett being taken hostage. Killian had snuffed out so many lives in his years of working for Killer of Kings that he had lost count of them. The men he killed all had it coming. He didn't like the evil that was in the world, and anyone who hurt a woman, well, that shit didn't settle well with him.

Boss had killed women, and it was something that Killian couldn't do. Growing up in Ireland to a mother who worked on the streets, bringing back all kinds of men, he'd seen the lowest of the low. The scum had hurt his mother, and when he was a little lad, he couldn't do a fucking thing about it. The nights after she had fucked her way through scores of men were the worst. Her pimp would arrive to take his piece of her pie, which was a large fucking piece, considering the man didn't spread his ass wide to take some of those johns. It had really fucked with Killian's head.

The pimp had done nothing to help his mother. She worked on his turf, and gave him money. The asshole wasn't there to protect her or to stop the johns from abusing her. All he did was take money, use her when he wanted, or pass her around like it was some kind of sport. Killian had hated that piece of shit. Every time he saw him, he vowed to take him out, and when the pimp had beaten his mother to death, it had been Killian who had found her body.

He'd been fighting, trying to earn enough money to stop his mother from whoring herself out. Holding her bleeding corpse in his arms, the rage had taken hold of him. All he wanted was blood, and he'd gone in search of that pimp.

By the time Killian was done with that asshole, there was nothing left of him. For seventy-two hours, Killian had taken sixteen years of pain out of that fucker, and made him pay. Every scream, every whimper, every cry had been a mark off the bastard's debt as far as he was concerned.

In all of his career, he had never, not once, harmed a woman until Scarlett. He hadn't touched that woman in any way, but he also hadn't stopped Boss either.

"Nothing was ever going to happen to Scarlett. I told you that," said Boss.

"I don't care. I need a break. I'll call you when I'm ready to take on assignments."

"Just tell me where you are."

"Like you don't know already? I'm in another lifetime." He disconnected the call and turned the device off completely. That was his only connection to Killer of Kings, to Boss. He wanted no part of it, not right now. Staring out across the ocean, he could almost hear her from over ten years ago.

Like all of the guys he worked with, he had a history. Not as fucked up as some, but it still hadn't been a picnic. He'd joined Killer of Kings when he was twenty years old, quite young all things considered.

After killing his mother's pimp, he'd killed everyone who ever laid a hand on her and caused her pain. He'd gotten the fuck out of there and made his way to the Americas. From there, he had done a great deal of fighting while also living on the streets. He'd lived it rough, and in the underground fighting circuit, he'd made a name for himself. That name had caught the attention of Boss, who had then trained him into the man he was today.

Killing people was something Killian was good at. He considered it an art form, and he was constantly getting it right.

Breathing in some of the fresh salty air, he allowed himself to think about *her*. The woman who had made him consider what he was doing. Ten years ago, he'd been twenty-six and on an assignment.

He'd been asked to tail this crime lord, and report back his findings to Boss, and only then would he be given details on what the final mission was. Killian couldn't remember the man he'd ended up killing, but

June he remembered. She was the one woman who'd been so innocent, too naive.

Watching her, being around her, had reminded him of the purity of life. When he was with her, he could pretend that he was just a college kid. He'd lied to her about everything. His age, his job, what he did, his past. Every single detail of his life had been nonstop lies. He didn't know how to be anything else.

June deserved better, and after tasting her sweetness for a few short weeks, he'd been sure to leave her to get on with her life.

Ten years had passed since he'd last seen her. Where he stood, in this very spot, was where he had first met her. She had been walking along with friends. The sand had been so dry that as she walked, she'd tripped. If he hadn't caught her, she'd have ended up with her face flat in the sand.

He smiled just thinking about that memory.

She'd fallen into his arms, and one look in her grey eyes, and he'd never wanted to look back. Many people believe in love at first sight. Before June, he'd believed it was a pile of bollocks.

After catching her, staring into her eyes, he'd known that it was very real.

He snorted to himself, thinking about how pathetic he sounded. She was probably pleased to be done with him. He imagined her being the CEO of an important company or something like that. Maybe married with 2.5 kids and the whole fucking white picket fence deal.

Not a moment went by when he wasn't tempted to go and look for her. Only his lies kept him at bay. He'd never told her the truth.

The story he'd woven had been everything he'd wanted in the past growing up.

He doubted she was still here, but he'd wanted to remember better times. After what he'd done, he wanted to be somewhere where he hadn't fucked up. When the memories were much better for him.

"Come here, you little shit!"

Killian frowned, and glanced toward the pier. He saw one man chasing after a little boy who couldn't be a day over ten years old.

"Come here now!"

"Fuck you. I didn't do nothin'."

The little kid had a bad attitude that was for sure.

The large guy finally caught up with the kid just as they exited the pier. The kid was grabbed by the scruff of his neck.

"I've told you before that I don't want your sort at my venue. Piece of thieving shit."

"I didn't take nothing, you fat twat. Let me go."

"Your mother should be ashamed of you."

"Yeah, well, you can't do nothin'. Let me go." The kid kicked the guy in the nuts, which meant he dropped to the floor.

Women and kids were Killian's limit. When he saw the guy about to take a swipe at him, he couldn't stand back and watch that.

"What is it the kid's done?" Killian asked.

The guy looked at him, and then at the kid. "Is this a fucking joke?"

"Watch your language."

"Then watch your kid more closely. Good for nothing, the lot of you."

The man shoved the kid into his arms, and Killian stared down … at himself. He stared at the kid, and was taken aback. Just looking at this boy and he could have sworn he'd gone back in time.

"Get off me," the kid said.

"What's your name?"

"Why do you want to know? You a perv? Want to take me somewhere, treat me special and fiddle with me? My friends told me about your kind."

Killian had had just about had enough of this kid's language. "I'm not a damn perv. Now tell me, what's your name?" He grabbed his arms, bent down, and gave him the best stern look he could.

The kid recoiled. "Killian, my name is Killian."
Holy shit!

He couldn't believe what was happening right now. There was only one person who would name her son after him, and it was the very woman he'd been thinking about less than a minute ago.

"Is your mother's name June?"

"Yeah, what's it to you? Are you one of her family that hates her because of me?" he asked.

"What?" Killian shook his head. "Take me to your mother now."

"Oh man, do we have to go? I'm sorry. I don't want no trouble."

"I'm not looking to get into any trouble. Take me to your damn mother now." There was no denying that this boy was his. It was like looking into his past, and he'd spent a lot of time growing up, staring at himself. He'd always wondered who his father was. With a whore for a mother, she'd told him it could be anyone.

He had promised himself that he would never father children, and yet there was one right before him.

Killian Junior led the way, and Killian senior was fucking nervous. Ten years had passed, and from what he just saw, the life he thought June had clearly wasn't the case.

****

June was going to throttle her son, and then she

was going to yell, scream, and possible smother him with kisses. She had asked him to stay at their apartment until she was done waitressing. It was high tourism season, and it was the time she got to save up as much of her earning as possible. She wanted to make it a good Christmas, and to do that without getting into debt, required double shifts, and often triple shifts.

Working at the diner was the only place that offered steady work outside of the seasons, and meant she could have some semblance of a life, or at least keep her son out of trouble, and away from some of the street gangs that were around nowadays.

He had to be at one of his friends or something. She would go three doors down, and make sure he was there before calling the police. Marching toward the door, she flung it open, and came face to face with her past.

"Killian," she whispered.

For several seconds neither of them spoke, nor moved. Her heart began to race as she stared at the man, who had aged gracefully. She'd spent months after finding out she was pregnant trying to find this very man. A man who had lied to her about the college he went to, the job he was working. Every little detail she had remembered that he'd told her had been a lie. That was what this man did, he lied.

"June," he said.

"Hey, Mom. He says he's not a perv? So I thought I'd bring him home."

"Why are you speaking in an English accent?" she asked.

"Told ya, Mom, guys don't mess with the Brits. Think of that spy I've seen on the telly."

She closed her eyes and wished the floor could open her up.

"I've got a kid," Killian said.

Ignoring the big Killian, she bent down, and looked at her son. "Will you do me a huge favor? Go to your room and finish your homework." When he went to complain, she pressed a finger against his lips. "You do that and I won't drag you to work with me next week, and make you do more than your homework. I'll make you clean grease for the entire five hours."

"Oh, Mom."

"Go. Homework. Now."

Killian went to his room, and she held onto the door. "You do not need to be here," she said.

"Excuse me, but that is my son."

"He's not your son. You have no claim over him whatsoever. Don't even for a second think you can come here, and make some stupid claim." Pain unlike anything she had ever felt before struck her hard. This man, she had given him everything. Her body, her heart, everything. She had loved him more than anything in the world. One day she'd woken up to discover him gone, and was told he would never return, that she had to move on with her life.

She'd tried to move on, and when it had started to work, the morning sickness happened. The pregnancy test happened, and finally, being thrown out by her parents, kicked out of college, and hitting rock bottom had also happened. Staring at Killian, as much as she was excited to see him, the pain held her back.

She went to close the door, and with very little effort, he pushed it open, and allowed himself back into her apartment. Where she lived was the best she could afford. The furniture was well used, second-hand. She tried her hardest to keep the smell of damp out of her place, and nights of praying she didn't live near drug dealers filled her life. This was so far from the ideal life she had hoped for.

Clenching her hands into fists, she stared at him as he closed the door with him inside her apartment.

"What do you want?" she asked, folding her arms. If she didn't keep herself together, she was going to attack him and not stop.

Killian looked around her apartment, and she saw the judgement in his eyes.

"This is where you live?"

"Yes."

"That boy, it's mine?"

"It's? He, Killian, yes, and he's your son." She gritted her teeth together, and took a deep breath. "Why are you here?"

"What happened to college?" he asked, avoiding her question.

"They didn't like knocked up candidates in their classroom, and then screaming babies cramp the studying environment." That was what the principal had told her. She had been let go, and her scholarship had gone to someone else. Her son was the best thing that had happened to her. She loved him more than anything, and never told him any different.

"Where are your parents?"

"You really don't get it, do you?" she asked. Even though ten years had passed, he seemed to think her life hadn't changed. "They wanted nothing to do with me. I've been alone, Killian. The only person I've got is Killian."

"And what a great job you're doing with him. His language is fucking awful."

She laughed. "Seriously, you're going to come here out of the blue, and start yelling at me? You want to judge me for what happened?"

He turned his back toward her, and began pacing. "This is not what you were supposed to have. You were always meant to have something more. You had college, an entire life in front of you."

She looked around her small space, and up until he'd criticized it, she had thought that she'd been doing really well. Every spare moment she worked to give her Killian a better life.

"I'm doing fine. You can leave, Killian. I don't know why you're even here, but whatever it is, I don't need you."

"Don't need me? You're living in a shithole with my son. You think for a second this is okay? Why the fuck didn't you reach out to me? I could have provided for you, and given you all the help you n—"

All of her life she had been the calm person, the respectful one. She rarely raised her voice, and the cops had even told her she wasn't hard enough on her son. Everything she had been through, from the loneliness, the hard labor, and everything in between. The men at the diner who had offered her more cash for her to suck their cock, or to let them fuck her ass. She'd had to grow up fast, and drop any notion of life being easy.

She had turned men down politely, even as they made her skin crawl. Everything she had gone through, and Killian thought it was fixed with just a phone call.

Picking up the nearest lamp, which had so many chips in it, she launched it at him. He didn't have time to catch it as it slammed into his middle. Next, she grabbed a coaster and threw it at him.

"Provided for me? Do you even know what I went through? The moment I found out, I tried to find you! But you know what, Killian? You were nowhere to be found. There was no contact information for you at your college, at your job. You completely vanished into thin air, so don't you fucking dare for a second try to turn this on me. I tried to find you. I was eighteen, the love of my life had just left me without any reason, and then I was pregnant. I was terrified!" She yelled the last part, and tears spilled down her cheeks.

For months, even years, she had thought about this moment so many times. In her fantasies, they had all been a lot nicer, a lot easier to deal with. They had talked, and everything had been fine.

Wrapping her arms around herself, she stared at the man who had broken her in more ways than she had thought possible. This was the man who had changed her life in ways she hadn't been able to comprehend at the time.

He stared at her, and neither of them spoke. She was panting, and trying her hardest not to fall apart. Nausea filled her, and finally, she turned her back on him, needing to go and see her Killian.

Standing in the doorway of her son's bedroom, he was reading his book.

"I love you, Mom," he said.

"Oh, honey, I love you, too."

So much. More than you can ever know.

Chapter Two

Killian had come here to clear his head, and never expected this revelation. All these years he'd had a kid and didn't even know it. Years he'd missed out on. He was no different than his own father who'd fucked his mother and disappeared. He felt sick to his stomach. And pissed off with the world.

He looked around the apartment, and his gut did another flip. Over the past ten years, he'd lived on top of the world with more cash than he could spend. Killer of Kings was very lucrative, and now he was Boss's right-hand man used for personal security and priority hits. He'd never stopped thinking of June, but had honestly believed she'd moved on with her life. The belief had both comforted him and torn him to shreds. Now he'd discovered she'd been slumming it in a piece of shit apartment, all her dreams left behind.

And there was a kid. *His* kid.

Killian couldn't believe the past was on rewind, his own son struggling to survive with a single mother killing herself to put food on the table. He felt tears prick his eyes, his throat getting scratchy. His kid deserved better than he'd had it. Shit, he shouldn't be running the streets in hand-me-down clothes, stealing to survive.

But it was too late to make amends. Killian would never see him as a father. He would forever be a fucking stranger, the bastard who'd abandoned his mother. He paced the room more, feeling anxious and volatile. He wanted to be angry at June, but she was right. He'd left with no way to contact him. It was supposed to be a sacrifice on his part, giving her up so she could live a normal life, a good life. If he had known she carried his baby, he never would have walked away.

"You didn't tell him anything, did you?" she

asked.

He turned to find her back in the room with him. "Tell him what? That I'm his father?"

"Yeah. That."

"No, but is that a problem? He is my son, after all."

She shook her head. "You gave up that right when you left without a trace. I won't have you confusing him, hurting him. He'll just fall in love with you, and then you'll be gone. Trust me, I know how that feels."

"I didn't know you were pregnant. For God's sake, you can't pretend I don't exist. I just found out I was a father twenty minutes ago," he said.

"Well, I've been his mother and father for the past ten years. It hasn't been easy, but I managed. You know why, because I had no choice. Being a parent comes with a lifetime responsibility, but you wouldn't understand that, would you?"

His fists clenched at his sides. He felt like he was on trial for a crime he hadn't committed, and he'd done a lot of bad shit.

"Look, I haven't stopped thinking about you over the years. You're the reason I came back to this town. But this, a kid, I never imagined any of it. If I'd known things would have been different," he said.

"Let me guess, you wouldn't have come back at all? Don't worry, I don't want your child support. You're free to leave." She crossed her arms over her chest again, completely blocking him out.

So many nights he'd picture this moment, this reunion, and it sure turned out better than the reality.

"You're fucking impossible!" He walked over to her and braced a hand on each of her shoulders. "I want to help. I want to make things right."

"I can't do this. I won't have you play with

Killian's heartstrings … or mine." She shrugged him off and opened the door. "Pretend you never found us. You're good at that."

He stood in the doorway for a minute, staring at her. She hadn't changed much since she was an innocent eighteen year old, still a natural beauty—still stubborn. Her gray eyes held him captive as they always had. One thing he couldn't help but notice was how she'd matured into a woman, a woman with enough curves to make his dick take notice. Just looking at her now, he struggled to take his eyes off her. She had a big, juicy set of tits, that there was no hiding. She had a rounder stomach, and even her thighs looked thicker. He didn't mind. This was his woman.

But he didn't like how tired she looked, dark circles under her eyes, the zest he remembered snuffed out. This life could do that to a person, he knew that firsthand. He'd watched his own mother waste away, her hard reality stripping her essence layer by layer until she was a shell of a woman.

Killian wanted to make things right, to give her back that sparkle, to make her dreams come true.

He wasn't going to fight her on this, not when they were both strung out on emotions. "If you think this is over, you're wrong. I'll never leave my son."

"Goodbye, Killian." She slammed the door on his ass. He wanted to punch his fist through it.

He noted the apartment number and the full address before he went back to his car. The ocean no longer held interest. He had a load of shit to think about.

Killian drove around the town, half in a daze. It hadn't improved over the years. In fact, it had gotten worse. He parked at the best-looking motel he could find, and got a room for a couple nights. As soon as he got his key and settled in, he called Maurice, one of the guys he used for occasional intel.

"I need some information. Fast," he said as soon as Maurice answered.

"Um, who's speaking?"

He exhaled, his patience still back in that apartment. "It's Killian. I need you to give me everything you can find on June Harris, twenty-eight, and her kid, Killian Harris."

"*Killian*? There something I should know?"

"Just get me the details. This needs to take priority," Killian said.

"I'll see what I can pull up. Should I send it to the same account?"

"Yeah. Thanks, Maurice." He hung up the phone, not in the mood to chitchat or to explain the shitty situation he'd gotten himself in. It was embarrassing. He wasn't a fucking deadbeat. He'd never planned on having any kids, but knowing he had a little boy changed everything.

He crashed back on the bed, the springs whining. How many miles had been put on this mattress? The ceiling had leak stains, and he tried to discover patterns in the yellow blotches. He closed his eyes, taking calming breaths.

When June said she'd had no one all these years, it tore him apart. He knew what if felt like to have no one and nothing. His roots were humble to say the least, but his harsh childhood had formed him into the man he was today. The only regret he really had was not being able to save his mother—that would fuck with his head until the day he died.

His phone vibrated.

He logged into his private server and opened Maurice's email. The man was a god behind a computer, and had saved his ass more times than he could count.

There were pages of information, overloading his head with guilt and anger. Everything June had told him was the truth. She also hadn't married or had any common law relationships. He expected lies from everyone because that's what he usually fell back on. Killian had started his white lies in public school, telling his friends about his fine home in the country, and the parents who loved and spoiled him. The truth had always been a bastard he wanted no part of.

The information on his son was more disturbing. He'd been involved with the cops, petty stealing, fights at school, and running away. The little fucker must have put June through the same hell he'd put his own mother through. He needed a father to set him straight, and in this case that responsibility fell on him.

Tomorrow he'd visit June with a level head. Tonight he needed a pub to forget absolutely everything.

****

June began her usual chores around the house, doing the dishes from last night, gathering up the laundry to bring to the laundromat tomorrow, and wiping down the dinette from breakfast. She moved like a robot, her heart still racing. She couldn't think about this now, think about *him*. Tears were a luxury she learned to hold back for the sake of her son. She refused to let him see how broken she was most nights, wanting nothing more than to cry herself to sleep. But they shared the only bedroom and she had to ensure his happiness.

She didn't know what she'd tell Killian Junior when he finished his homework. And he'd ask. That boy was smart, and he'd know something wasn't right.

Tonight she'd taken an extra shift at one of the local pubs, so a babysitter was coming once Killian was in bed. She hated paying for childcare, but she had no choice. The little money she'd clear was still better than nothing, and tips on closing shift were usually the best.

June began putting the clean dishes away. Her body, mind, and soul were tired. She'd imagined Killian coming back for her, like her knight in shining armor. He'd love her, take care of her, and they'd live happily ever after like in the fairytales. But June had given up on dreams so many years ago. She'd given up on Killian returning.

When she first saw him, she knew it was her lost love. She'd never forget his face.

Although she'd recognize him anywhere, he'd roughened around the edges. He looked damn good, and it pissed her off that she was even more attracted to him now than over a decade ago. He had a five o'clock shadow, his dirty-blond hair shaved at the sides and long at the top. Those intense blue eyes still made her knees weak.

"Mom?"

She gasped, pulled from her thoughts. June turned to face her son. "Yes?"

"That man knew you. Who was he?"

"Just an old friend, sweetheart."

He tilted his head to the side. "A boyfriend?"

She shook her head. "Never you mind that," she said, changing the subject. "I'm going to prepare dinner, so help me set the table. I have a lot to get done before work."

"You just got home from work."

June sighed, squatting down to Killian's level. God, he looked like his father. She kept her emotions in check. "We've been through this. I need to work extra for a few months, but you won't even notice I'm gone. Melissa will be here while you're asleep, but I'll be here when you wake up." She kissed his forehead.

"Don't you need to sleep, Mom?"

She winked. "Mommies don't need sleep. We're like superheroes." June chuckled as she shuffled Killian off to do his chores. Tonight she'd make some macaroni and cheese. It would fill them up enough for the night.

By the time Melissa showed up at her door, Killian was tucked into their bed. June hoped he'd stay there. In the past six months he'd tried to run away twice when he had a babysitter. She knew he was rebelling because her time with him was spread thin, and it pissed her off she couldn't be there for him like she wanted.

She got off the bus twenty minutes later, her feet already tired. At twenty-eight she felt more like sixty-eight. Her mind wanted to drift to fantasies of Killian, but she shoved them away, refusing to fall victim to his whims again. She still hadn't gotten over the fact he could walk away from what she considered the love of a lifetime. But she really didn't know him at all. He'd been so sweet and attentive, an arts student at the local college, and working part-time in a local hardware store—only he wasn't.

Shit, she was thinking about him and now her mood had soured before she even started her shift. It was bad enough she'd have to deal with all the filthy perverts as they drank too much and felt they had a right to touch or proposition her.

After an hour on the floor, June was running around tending all the customers. The place was packed, which was good for tips but bad for potential problems. This place wasn't exactly a 5-star lounge. It was a sketchy drinking hole for the worst of the worst. She'd only gotten the job because she was blessed in the bosom department, but she wasn't going to turn down the second job when she desperately needed the money. June just did her best to mind her business and stay off the radar.

"Hey, fun cheeks, give me a kiss, eh?" A man

patted his lap, waiting for her to sit down.

She leaned away from the bearded man. He was one of the higher ups in a local MC. That still didn't mean she was on the menu. "Maybe you've had enough to drink?" she suggested.

He scowled, grabbing her t-shirt and tugging her towards him. His friends stood around him, laughing. She was nothing, garbage, usable—and she wanted to cry. She wanted to be cuddled up to her son in their little apartment. She wanted more. But she was here, and she was powerless.

"Let me go!" she said. "You have no right." Her tears were so close to the surface, but she had to appear stronger than that.

"I own this town," he said, the scent of alcohol on his breath stinging her eyes.

She shook her head, struggling. Her bastard boss didn't even attempt to help her because he was terrified of the Dead Angels MC. They'd torn his bar up numerous times when he didn't let them have their way.

"I think the lady said to let her go."

They all turned to the voice. It was Killian. He was dressed in black, his hair slicked back from his face. There was no hint of fear or emotion in his eyes. As much as she was relieved to see him, he'd get himself killed standing up to these men.

"And why the hell do you care, pretty boy?"

"Because that's my woman."

There were gasps and chuckles in the bar. Killian hadn't moved an inch, even as the gang member started to circle him.

"Killian, just go. I don't want you to get hurt," said June. She tried to hate him, but she'd always love him.

He smiled, curling a finger motioning her to

come. "I want you to wait for me outside, baby."

"I'm on shift until three," she said.

"No, I promise, you're done working at this shithole. Now wait outside." His tone left no room for argument. She reluctantly walked toward the entrance, turning back the entire time. If she had a cell phone, she'd call the cops.

"You put your hands on her," said Killian. "That was your first fucking mistake."

"Really, what're you gonna do about it, pretty boy?"

He cracked his head to each side, then his knuckles. "I'm going to fuck you up."

Killian moved so fast, she almost missed it. With one short straight punch to the face, the bearded man fell off his stool to the floor, out cold. Killian moved like a professional boxer, ducking away from every blow and delivering devastating punches to the other men, one at a time. They dropped like flies, and June couldn't believe her eyes.

When one of the men pulled out a handgun, she froze, too scared to move or scream in warning.

The old bastard chuckled, aiming at Killian. "Not so tough now are you, blondie?"

"You call that a fucking gun? No, these are guns." Killian reached both arms behind him, and returned with a gun in each hand, pointing at two different men.

"Do you know who we are?"

Killian scoffed. "You're assholes who messed with the wrong woman." Then he fired, the sound impossibly loud. June slapped her hands over her ears and squatted down. She closed her eyes, listening to gunshots ring out. When silence finally settled, she peeked open her eyes. Killian was the only one standing. He holstered those two guns and then casually pulled out his wallet. He slapped a wad of cash on the bar. "To help with the damage, not that you deserve it for letting lowlifes like these in here."

He approached her, and she wasn't sure if she should be scared or not. She didn't know this new Killian at all.

"You killed them," she whispered.

"No, they're all alive and well. Each with a reminder not to fuck with me." He took her hand and left the bar. "Trust me, he's lucky. I wanted to put a bullet right between that piece of shit's eyes."

Once they were on the street, walking away from the bar, reality rained down on her, painful and harsh. "My job. I lost my job because of you."

He scowled down at her, no other expression on his face. "Is that how little you think of yourself, June? You think it's okay to let scum like that have their way with you?"

"I have no choice!"

"Do you sell yourself, too?"

Rage built up inside her so strong that she started to beat on his chest with the little strength she had left. All these years, she'd had opportunities to sell her body or give one of those monsters a lap dance, but she'd always refused. There were some lines she refused to cross. "You bastard! I hate you!"

"Whoa there." He easily subdued her, holding her wrists against his chest.

"Why don't you kill me, too?"

He exhaled in a growl, then hoisted her up into his arms. How had he gotten so strong? She was no lightweight. June wanted to struggle, but she was so spent, so weary of life. For once it would be so nice to have someone to lean on.

"My job," she muttered.

"Get over it, baby. You're never setting foot in that place again. Things are going to change around here, starting with this hate you have for me."

They got to a car, and he set her down on her feet. It was a silver Porsche with chrome rims that shone under the streetlights. She didn't know much about cars, but recognized the logo.

"Is this your car?"

He pulled out his key fob and clicked open the door with one push. "I'm taking you to my hotel room. It's sketchy as fuck, but it's the best I could find in this town."

"I need to go home. Killian needs me."

"No, little Killian's fast asleep, or he better be. Right now, we have some unfinished business to deal with. I never should have left you, but I'm back, and I'm not leaving." He cupped the back of her neck and leaned down. "You're mine."

Then he kissed her.

Chapter Three

For a few precious seconds, June allowed herself to be transported back ten years ago, where life was simple. There were times she missed her old life—the dreams she'd had, the fantasies. Every second she had been with Killian ten years ago, she felt like she'd found her soul mate. It had all been a lie. Nothing had been true, so she pulled away from the kiss, shoving him hard in the process.

"I'm going home, and I'm going to figure out the mess that you've gotten me into. I don't know who you are." Before she even made it a couple of steps, he grabbed her arms and hauled her into his car. Within seconds he had her strapped in and the car door locked. When she pulled on the handle, it wouldn't budge. The child lock had been put on. Her day was going from bad to worse. "Let me go."

"You seem to think that I give a fuck what you want right now," Killian said, climbing behind the wheel. "Newsflash, sweetheart. I'm not going anywhere. I'm not disappearing, and I sure as shit am not walking away again. I did that once, and it was a fucking nightmare. I'm not going to do it again."

She shook her head, and stared out of the window. This was not what she wanted to do.

"Take me home. I mean it, Killian. If I'm not working then I want to be with him."

"We need to talk."

"We can talk at my house. I'll even make you a coffee. How's that? Do you think that's reasonable?" She didn't like how bitchy she sounded, but the truth was, she didn't know what to do. Part of her wanted to run, jump into his arms and pretend the last ten years hadn't happened. That she didn't find out he was nothing like he had said. Everything he'd told her had been nothing but lies. She couldn't pretend. Her life wouldn't let her. Her son wouldn't let her.

The time for fairytales ended a long time ago.

"You're not going to call the cops on me? Try and cause me a few problems?" he asked.

"Are you a wanted man?"

He threw his head back and laughed. "No, baby. I'm not a wanted man."

"Stop calling me baby. I'm no one's baby."

"No, you're someone's mom."

"I'm our son's mom," she said. This was just too much for her. "Please, take me home."

"Fine. I'll take you home, but you can't get rid of me. You don't like it, and I get it, but we do have to talk."

She watched the dark scenery go by. "You know I've thought about this moment a lot. At first when I found out I was pregnant, I figured you'd come back, and I'd tell you. Everything would be fine."

"I never came back."

"You never came back, and then I couldn't leave. There's a lot of seasonal work here. Killian, our son, he loves the ocean, or he did."

"I read pretty hard shit about him."

She stared at him, waiting for more.

"Been caught by the cops for some petty crap," Killian said.

"I don't know how you've got that information, but I don't like it. It's nothing. Just some trouble that he's getting into. He's at that age, acting out." She ran fingers through her hair. This was a topic she hated more than anything.

The first time two cops had come to her door as they'd held Killian by the scruff of his neck. Since then she'd had a social worker involved, the school, pretty much anyone who wanted to take Killian away, had been in touch.

She loved her son more than anything else in the world, and she couldn't, wouldn't live without him.

Killian parked outside of her apartment block, and she felt his judgment coming off him in waves.

"I still can't believe your parents didn't help you out."

"To them I was nothing more than a whore. I ruined myself by being with you. No scholarship, no family, and I was alone. All I had was that little boy. This is the best I can afford. I'm working all the hours I can to get us better. I'm trying." She opened the car door, and began to walk away from him. She didn't like how he made her feel.

She needed to pay Melissa and to stop thinking about another lifetime. This man wasn't the sweet guy she had once known. She'd just watched him shoot men in front of her very eyes. From what she'd heard they were very dangerous men, and yet Killian had killed them with ease. No way were those warning shots. She'd seen the blood and carnage with her own eyes.

Her gut was telling her that she wasn't going to like hearing the truth about him. They were no longer in a fairytale but in sobering real life.

Killian didn't let her get far before he grabbed her arm and spun her around. "That boy needs his father, June."

She couldn't cry. Refused to cry. "I've been everything for my son. I'm doing my best, Killian. Do you even know what it's like to be a single mother? To have to put your kid into the care of neighbors while you work?"

"I know more about it than you can even imagine."

"Yeah, right." She made to pull away, but he wouldn't let her.

"My mother was a whore," he said, suddenly.

Looking into his eyes, she didn't know if that was the truth. Or if he was being an asshole. "You told me your parents were self-employed back in Ireland."

"They never were. My mother sold her body to every single man that would take her. She had a pimp. I didn't have a clue who my father was, still don't."

Tears filled her eyes. "You think this makes me feel better? You lied to me. Everything you told me back then was nothing but lies. How do I even know what's real or not?"

Killian pulled her close, cupping her cheek. "My feelings for you, that's what was real. Every single feeling that we had together, that was all real."

Damn it!

It would be so easy to fall into his embrace. To forget the damage of the past few years, but she couldn't do it.

"I don't even know you." She pulled away. "I don't know anything about you. What you do? Why you were here ten years ago? Why you never looked back? I waited for you, you know. I'd go to the beach every single day, getting bigger and bigger, and yet you still didn't come back."

"I had no idea you were pregnant, June. I swear to you, I would have come back." She snorted at that. "I left because I didn't for a second believe that I was good enough for you. Still don't. You're right. I've got a lot of secrets. I don't talk about myself, and to be honest, I never wanted to. I've never had the proud parents, or the perfect life. No one's waiting for me when I go home. There's nothing for me."

"I don't know what to say." She began walking

back to her apartment. There were so many questions. So much confusion. She wanted to tell him to fuck off and to stay at the same time. Everything was all muddled in her head.

June wasn't a naïve virgin anymore, loving the attention of this sexy man who noticed her.

Twenty-eight years old, single, with a child, tired all the time, and watching her son grow up, knowing she didn't spend enough time with him—that was the life she had, and she hated it.

This was never her plan. Her future had been bright, but that seemed like a lifetime ago.

Entering her apartment, she saw Melissa sitting on the sofa. She was reading from her textbook, which she immediately began putting away the moment she saw her.

"Hey, June. You're back early."

"Sorry. Something came up, but I'm home now. How has he been?"

"Really good. He went to the toilet earlier, and straight back to bed. Everything was fine."

"Excellent, thank you, sweetie."

She paid Melissa, and waited for her to leave the apartment.

"You have people babysit him? He's ten," Killian said.

"Still too young to be left alone, and he gets into way too much trouble without even trying." She took a breath. "I'll go and check on him. If you want to put the kettle on, we can talk."

She didn't give him the chance to argue as she made her way toward the room she shared with Killian. Opening the door slightly, she glanced over, and frowned. Flicking the light on, she moved toward him, and there where her son should be was a damn pillow.

This was not the first time he'd done this. And each time was as scary as the first.

Leaving the room, she looked over at Killian senior.

"He's gone!" She rushed toward the door.

"What do you mean he's gone?"

"He's not in his bed. He's done this several times. I've got to go and look for him."

"I'm coming, too."

They left the apartment, and she made sure to lock the door. She didn't pretend to live in a good area. Running down the staircase, they exited the building

"It'll be faster if we split up. He normally wears this jacket with a hood on. Please, find him." She didn't want to hear anything else. She had to find her son.

****

Nothing was going according to plan. It was one fuck up after another, and Killian was getting pissed off. Every second he spent with June was just another pain in his heart because he'd left her and caused this mess. Everything he'd done was with the intention to help her, and yet it had been totally the opposite, and he was so fucking angry about that.

He had a son.

A little boy.

Never for a second could he have imagined being a daddy. Well, he had thought about it before Killer of Kings became part of his life. He'd vowed to be a better father than his own. To always be there, to provide, to love, to nurture. Instead, he'd knocked her up, and abandoned her. She had been fighting every single day.

Maurice had sent him all the details about June Harris. All of the jobs she'd had, the time sheets she'd done. That woman had done nothing but work for the past ten years.

His cell phone started to ring, and he glanced down to see it was Boss. Since calling Maurice, Killian had kept his cell phone on. His intention had been to get away from the damn job, but now Boss was calling, and he had no choice but to answer.

"What?"

"Is that anyway to talk to your boss?"

He rolled his eyes as Boss began to chuckle. "What do you want?"

"I thought you needed some time away."

"I did. Look, I don't have time for this shit, Boss. I need to go."

"Well, you see, I've got a bit of a problem here."

"Why?" Killian asked.

"Because a hit has just gone live on June and Killian Harris. Now you see my confusion." Killian paused. Boss had his attention. "Now at first I thought that hit was for you. Killian and all. But it just so happens that the details I have on my desk are for a twenty-eight-year-old woman, and a ten-year-old boy. Then I talk to Maurice, and he had the same request for information from you. What the hell is going on here, Killian?"

"Why the hit?" Killian asked.

"Why the hit indeed. It's because of you. Someone must be watching you, or waiting."

"Find out who took the hit. Boss, don't put anyone onto this, please." Boss never could turn down money. "That's my kid. I've only just found him, and she's my girl. I just … I fucked up. I need time to fix this."

Silence fell.

"Killian, I know I'm a monster, or at least a lot of people believe I'm a monster. I have my reasons for doing what I do."

"And no one else fucking gets that."

Boss had a lot of secrets. He wasn't an easy man to please. In fact, he was downright difficult at times.

"It's my kid, and I fucked up. As a favor to me. You owe me, Boss."

"Again, I had no intention of taking this hit, Killian. Until I find out who ordered this contract, she's in danger. I suggest you find them. This kill went live an hour ago."

Killian paused. Was it because of the men he tried to make an example of?

Either way, he didn't know what to fucking do. Disconnecting the call, his heart was racing. What the fuck had he done?

This was becoming one clusterfuck after another.

He picked up the pace, walking down a long street, and then heading toward the pier where he'd first met the kid. Little Killian was there, hands in his pockets, looking out at the ocean.

"You know your mom is having the fright of her life right now?" He wasn't doing too well either.

Fuck, fuck, fuck.

"She's always working. Always away. Each job she gets that has decent pay, never lasts. Nothing ever lasts," Killian said.

Gone was the British accent, and the cocky attitude. There before him was his son. From what he'd just said, the kid missed his mom. He was hurting.

Killian stared out at the view. There was a kill out on this kid, and his woman. He'd totally fucked up.

"Your mother does everything she does because she has to."

"I know she does. She's always tired, and I don't care that she thinks she's a superhero. They don't exist. Nothing exists but work and bills. She wants me to go to school, get my education, and go to college. Only rich kids get to do that. Not someone like me. I want to make her proud, but I don't have it in me to do that."

"Your mom is worried about you. You weren't in your bed."

"She came home?" Killian Junior asked.

"She came home, and she went to check on you, and began to panic."

"Crap. I was going to make it back home. I told her I wouldn't do this again. I just … ugh. I wanted her to stay at home. I don't get to see her anymore. I don't care about Christmas gifts. I know there's no Santa! I just want her home. It's what I told that social worker lady that came to my school. The lady warned me that I'm getting into a lot of trouble, and if I want to leave my mom, then it will only be a matter of time before I'm taken away. I don't want to leave my mom. I love her."

This kid reminded him so much of himself it was unreal.

Already his past was starting to come back full circle. A mother that worked all the time. A lost boy. June didn't sell her body, so at least his own son didn't have to see the beatings that the johns gave.

"Your mom is going to be spending a lot of time with you from now on."

"How do you know?"

"Because I'm going to be taking care of the both of you. You'll get to spend every single second with her, and no one will be taking her away from you."

Killian Junior stared at him. "How do you know my mom?"

"I know her from the past."

"Yeah, but when? I talked to my mom, and she said you were from a long time ago."

"I am." His son was staring at him, assessing him. It was so surreal to know that he helped create this little boy.

"How long?"

"Roughly ten years ago and a few extra months." He shoved his hands into his pockets. "I'm your father, Killian. We even share the same name."

"We do? Your name's Killian as well?"

"Yes. My name is Killian. You mother named you after me."

"Well, where the fuck have you been?" Killian Junior asked. "I've been waiting for you since I was five years old."

"Why five?" he asked.

"I asked for you on the wish of my birthday cake. Those are supposed to come true, and you never came. You never turned up to help my mom, you asshole."

"Watch your damn language."

"You don't deserve my mom, and she should get rid of you." Killian Junior stormed away from him, and this was not how he expected this to go either.

"I didn't know about you," he said, taking hold of his son's arm. "I know that doesn't give me the right to demand a second chance, but I'm asking for it." He was trying to reason with a ten year old. At ten years old, there was no reasoning for him, and now he was fucking everything up. "I didn't have a dad either, and no one came back to claim me. I want you and your mother. I want to get to know you and to hear everything I've missed. Your first day of school. Maybe the first time you tasted chocolate. I want to know every single thing about you. What's your favorite color? What do you want to be when you grow up? What is the worst thing you've done that you've been caught for?"

His son looked down at the ground.

"I want to know everything about you, Killian."

"A lot of the crap they say I did was lies. There

was a guy on the force who wanted to date my mom. Told him he didn't have a chance with my mom. He didn't like that I was there. I'm only extra baggage."

Killian didn't like the jealousy that rushed over him at the thought of anyone else liking his woman. She belonged to him, and only him.

"You're going to need to watch your language. I bet your mother doesn't like hearing you swear?"

"She doesn't, but I have to look out for her. If my mom hadn't overheard that cop telling me I was a waste of space and ruined my mother's life, she might have dated him, and that guy didn't deserve her. You don't deserve her either. You're never going to be good enough for my mom."

And that was the truth. Killian didn't deserve June ten years ago, and he sure as shit didn't deserve her now.

"I know, but I want to make myself worthy in your eyes, and in your mom's eyes. Do you think you'll give me that chance?" he asked.

His son pursed his lips, and then shrugged. "We'll see. Can't be any worse than what we've already had."

"Killian!" June shouted.

They both turned to see June had spotted them. She was rushing toward them, and he smiled. It didn't matter that ten years had passed. He still loved this woman just as strongly as he had back then, if not stronger.

Holding Killian's hand, he began to walk toward her, and then stopped at the unmistakable sounds of wheels braking. Spinning around, he watched as the black SUV's door opened, and there was a man with a gun. Pulling his son behind him, he watched in horror as the gun was aimed toward June.

There was nothing he could do. One lone shot rang out, and June fell down. Grabbing one of his guns, he pointed it toward the car, and began firing.

The SUV was gone before he landed a single bullet.

June was on the ground, and his son held him tightly. He'd brought his darkness back to the birthplace of his sweetest memories.

What had he done?

Chapter Four

Killian holstered his weapon and ran over to June, dropping to his knees beside her. He patted down her body, assessing the damage. There was fear in her eyes, pain and confusion. This was all on him.

"It's okay, baby. Everything's going to be okay." He prayed to God he could keep that promise.

"Mommy!" Little Killian was broken and crying, his arms around June's chest. The scene reminded him of that night he'd found his own mother dead. It gave him pause, his childhood horrors rushing to the surface. He pushed the memories away as he hoisted June up into his arms.

They weren't too far from the apartment complex, but no way in hell was he taking them home. Boss said there was a hit on June and the lad, so the place would be hot. These two people were now all that mattered, and they were his responsibility.

"Where we going?" asked Killian, chasing along beside him.

"Somewhere safe," he said.

When they got to his car, he asked his son to open the back door. He carefully laid June across the seats, instructing Killian to get in the front passenger side.

"Killian, I'm scared," said June.

He turned around in his seat after starting up the car. "I'll make sure you're never afraid again. I'm here, and I'm not going anywhere."

Killian left the seaside town without a backwards glance. He never wanted to see it again. Never wanted June or Killian to struggle in that shithole another day.

The highway was dark and quiet at this hour, the purr of the engine not enough to mask June's muffled sobs. His mind was on overdrive, piecing everything together, trying to figure out how to make things right. He couldn't do this alone. He needed Killer of Kings.

He pulled out his cell and called Boss. The bastard was as a hard ass, but he'd helped him get his start when he moved over from Ireland. They had an unorthodox relationship to say the least.

"Boss, I was too late, one of them shot June."

"She alive?"

"Yeah. I've got them both. Need a safe house for my boy until we can deal with the problem." As in fill those assholes with so much fucking lead even the coroner couldn't identify the bodies.

There was silence on the other end. "Take him to Bain and Scarlett's house. He'll be safe there."

"Any word on who set it up?"

"Still working on the details, but it's related to that Dead Angels kill from over a decade ago," said Boss.

"How the fuck is that possible? It was clean and handled."

Killian barely remembered that hit. He'd taken out the leader of the club after doing recon for a few weeks. It's when he met June, so all his memories centered on her.

"I'll be touch when I know more," said Boss.

As he continued driving to Bain's place in the country, he glanced over at little Killian. He was looking out the window, not saying a word. Killian wanted to make things better, not worse. He didn't want his own son to turn out as fucked up as he was.

He hated the idea of dropping his son off at someone else's place, but things were going to get ugly before they got better and he didn't want Killian hurt or exposed to more unnecessary violence. The outside lights were on as he drove down Bain's long driveway, so Boss must have filled him in. He stopped the car and turned to

June. She looked pale.

"Babe, I'm leaving Killian here for a while. Just until things settle down," he said.

"What? No! I'm not leaving him at a stranger's house. He needs to be with his mother."

"And he will be. When it's safe. I trust Bain with my life. Nothing will happen to Killian here, I promise."

She glared at him, and Killian knew it would be a long road before she trusted him again. He'd have to earn it, to make up for the mountain of lies he'd told in the past.

"Come on, Killian."

His son got out of the car without complaint. He was a brave kid. They walked hand in hand to the front door, and before they reached it, Scarlett opened it up. She smiled warmly at his son.

"You must be Killian Junior," Scarlett said, holding her rounded stomach. She looked to be at least a few months pregnant. "I've heard so much about you."

His son looked up at him, looking for reassurance. It was a step in the right direction. He had a lot of years to make up for. "It's okay. She's a friend. You'll be safe here."

"What about my mom?"

"I'm going to take care of her. And as soon as I fix this mess, I'm coming for you."

"You sure you'll come back this time? Or are you like that cop and want me out of the picture?"

He bent down on one knee to get on Killian's level. "I'll never leave you. You're not some random kid to me. You're my son. My blood. I want us to be a family, all three of us, not just me and your mom. Understand?"

He nodded, his jaw tight.

"Come on in, honey. I'll show you to your room.

You must be tired," said Scarlett.

She led little Killian upstairs.

Bain joined him in the entryway, his arms crossed. "You don't have to worry about the boy."

"I know."

"Scarlett's working on this shit, too. She found the Dead Angels MC tie in, but there's more she needs to dig up."

"Good. Great." He didn't know what to say. For the first time since starting his new life in this country, he felt a unique vulnerability. He'd been fucking unstoppable, fearless … feared. Now he had to rely on other people, and despite Boss's frequent warnings not to, he'd fallen in love. Twice. He'd do anything to keep June and Killian safe. "Apparently, he likes to run away, so you'll have to keep a—"

"I've got this, Killian. My place is like Fort Knox. Nobody gets in or out without my consent. I promise you that. If any of those assholes dares to pay a visit, I have a fucking arsenal ready to send them straight to hell."

"That's what I need to hear," Killian said. "I'm heading home. You have my number. June's injured, and I need to take care of that before anything else."

"And when you find out who's responsible?"

Killian smirked. "Let's just say it won't end well for them."

He got back into the car and drove towards the city. "We're almost there, June. Hang on for me."

"Why can't Killian come with us?" she asked. "I don't understand any of this."

"He's my son, too. I won't let anything happen to him. I'll explain everything, answer all your questions as soon as we get there."

"Get where?"

"My place."

When he saw the lights of the city come into view, he felt a measure of comfort. This was his playground, where he did most of his work for Killer of Kings. It was easy to disappear, and had enough distractions to take his mind off the girl he had to give up.

Only now he had her back. This time he wasn't letting her go.

He carried her through the front entrance of the lobby. The security guards nodded to him, allowing him to pass by without an interrogation. Boss had them on his payroll. Some nights Killian would come home with blood on his clothes, his weapons exposed, but he never had to worry about being reported.

"This place looks expensive," she said.

Killian was used to the best. Demanded it. After living the first half of his life in dire poverty, he enjoyed the finer things, including the penthouse suite with a view of the downtown core. "It is."

When he got to his suite, he managed to get the door open without putting June to her feet. He knew her injuries were minor or he else he would have treated her immediately. It was still way too close for his liking. She could have easily been seriously injured … or killed. He would never have been able to live with himself if she died because of his lifestyle.

He settled June down on one of his leather sofas and then turned on the lights. Killian was a fucking mess. He shrugged off his jacket and removed his handguns, placing them on the bar.

"You've got a flesh wound there, sweetheart. I don't know if that hitman was the world's worst shot, or just sending me a message." He sat on the coffee table in front of the sofa with his first aid kit. Boss didn't permit his men to use public doctors or hospitals—too many questions. Killer of Kings had their own underground doctors on call twenty-four, seven. For non-emergencies, they were responsible for their own medical care, including things like broken ribs and flesh wounds. Killian's emergency supplies were always well stocked.

He helped June get her sweater off. She cringed, moving her arm out of the sleeve in slow increments. "I can't believe I was shot," she said. "Why would someone want to shoot me?"

"Because I love you, and whoever did this wanted to hurt me. It's the reason my boss doesn't like any of us getting involved in serious relationships. That hasn't gone too well for him lately, considering I'm the third guy this year to put a woman first."

"Is that what you call this? Putting me first?" she asked.

He examined her upper arm. The bullet had just grazed her flesh, and he was thankful it hadn't been worse. "From now on, you and my son are number one." Killian used a disinfectant wipe around the area, and then dressed the wound. Her skin was fucking soft.

"And who is your boss exactly? I mean, what are you?"

Now that her wound had been tended, he couldn't help but notice the rest of June. She'd been wearing just a pink sports bra under her sweater, her big tits barely contained. Ten years ago she'd been a lot smaller, young and naïve. Now she'd filled out into a real woman, with a feistiness that kept him in check.

"I work for an organization called Killer of Kings. My job, it's complicated."

She struggled up into a sitting position, so he helped her, supporting her back. June did a visual sweep of the room. "It obviously pays well. What are you, a hitman?"

He licked his lips. She'd just been teasing, but her

guess was spot on. Killian was terrified June would push him away, want nothing to do with him if she knew the truth. But he couldn't lie. Not anymore.

"Yeah, something like that."

She narrowed her eyes, then shook her head. "That's not possible. You're lying again."

"Not this time, baby. I told you lies before because I had nothing good in my life, nothing to be proud of. You were a fantasy, so I conjured up what you wanted to hear."

"You don't know what I wanted to hear. What I wanted was the truth. Maybe if you had of been honest instead of telling me you were this straight A college boy, I wouldn't have been raising Killian alone for the past ten years."

"So if I told you I was born to a whore, raised on the streets, and fought and stole to survive, you'd be okay with it? What about getting hired by Killer of Kings when I moved over from Ireland, murdering people for a living? Would you still want me then?" He felt like a cornered dog, bristling but also embarrassed. He didn't want June to judge him.

She kept quiet, staring at him with no hint of what she was feeling on the inside. Was there any chance she could love him again?

****

June didn't know what to say, what to think. Killian had told her the truth this time, she just knew it. Besides, who would make up such wicked lies? She wanted to hate him, not just for abandoning her all these years, but for what he represented. He was a bad guy, a criminal, and he'd brought a whirlwind of danger into her life. Into her son's life.

But she loved him, completely and unconditionally. It pissed her off that she was turned on by the visual of Killian with guns in his hands. It was such a natural look for him. He'd aged like a fine wine, exuding strength and confidence. He could protect her, care for her, love her. It was all she'd prayed for all these years.

"Killian, you're the only man I've ever loved. I've never forgotten you. How could I? Your son has been a constant reminder. Even though I'd given up faith the past few years, part of me still hoped you come for me."

"I fucked up, but I promise I'll make things right. For the three of us." He got down to his knees and put his head on her lap. It was a vulnerable moment, this grown man, this killer, still a damaged boy on the inside. "Please, June. Just tell me you'll give me that chance. I have nothing else. I want nothing else."

She ran her hands through his hair, still in shock he was back in her life. So many scenarios had played in her head over the years from Killian being dead to being happily married.

"Why now, Killian? Why did you wait this long before coming back? I've never moved from town, so it's not like you couldn't find me."

"I thought I was doing the right thing. I'm a hitman for hire. You deserved better than that. Fuck, I wanted to be that college boy—for you. But I never even finished elementary school. I'm a fuck-up, but I promise no one will ever love you more than me."

It was too good to be true, and her emotions got the better of her. Her eyes welled up with tears, and when she blinked, they traced down her cheeks. "How will you take care of us? We can't continue like this. I don't want Killian living in fear."

He rose up on his knees, his hands still on her hips. Only now did she realize she was in her work bra, her sweater on the coffee table. What did he think of her?

A decade ago she'd been thin and young, her skin flawless. Now she had stretch marks, and a lot of extra weight. She was nothing like she used to be. Killian had only gotten sexier, packed on muscle, and to be honest, she couldn't stop imagining them in bed together.

"Just tell me one thing, baby girl. Tell me if you still love me, if there's a fucking chance you *could* love me again," he said.

She nodded, not trusting her voice with her emotions so fragile. The constant rejection and struggling over the years had taken their toll. This new desire, this acceptance from Killian was healing. "I'll always love you."

His blue eyes looked even bluer, and she expected him to break down. "That's all I needed to hear," he said. "You'll never have to worry about anything, June. You're going to have the best because I'm going to give it to you—you and my son. No more working, no more babysitters or raising that boy alone."

Killian leaned closer, his massive shoulders swallowing her up. He brushed his lips along hers, a low growl in his chest.

"I'm not the eighteen year old you remember," she whispered. June had never really given a shit what people, especially men, thought of her. Now she felt a new burden, and wondered if Killian was attracted to her.

"I don't want a girl, June. I'm a man, and I need a woman by my side. I need you."

She brought her arms around to hug her stomach. Her current position was not flattering, and being half-naked left her feeling uncomfortable.

"What are you doing?" he asked.

June pushed away from him and stood up, grabbing her sweater to use as a shield. She wandered around, taking in the state of art entertainment center, full bar, and museum-quality artwork. Every finish from the crown moldings to the light fixtures screamed money.

They were from two different worlds.

Back at home, they didn't even own a television set, and a six-dollar bottle of wine was as fancy as it ever got. She didn't buy new clothes or treat herself to nice things. Everything was about secondhand stores and sacrifices.

"Don't do this, June. Stop pulling away from me."

She had nothing to lose. If she returned to her old life, then she'd survive as she always did. "Killian, you've done well for yourself. Just because we have a kid together, doesn't mean we have to be a couple."

He charged over and grabbed both her arms in a firm grip. A darkness passed over his eyes as he stared at her. "What don't you get, woman? I've told you everything, spilled my fucking guts because I promised not to lie to you."

His accent was stronger when he was angry. It turned her on.

"I don't want you to settle for me. I want things to be like before, when I thought we had something special."

Killian chuckled. "You have no idea, babe. You're the only woman for me. The things I want to do your body right now…" He tossed her sweater and pulled her tight to his body, crushing his lips to hers. She closed her eyes and let everything go—the fear, the doubts, the resentment. God, he tasted good, like spearmint and raw masculinity. His cologne enveloped her, a rich musky scent that made her blood burn with need.

His hands roamed down, cupping her ass. She could feel the hardness of his cock against her stomach, and her pussy began to ache for him. "Killian," she murmured against his lips.

"Yeah, baby, say my name. I love the way it sounds coming from you." He trailed hot kisses down her neck, his hands roaming everywhere. "You're mine. And I'm going to claim you all over again, discover every inch of this beautiful body."

Chapter Five

June's curves were better than Killian even imagined. Just one look at her, and he'd been picturing her in his arms for the rest of the day. Of course whenever it came to June, he always thought about her, wanted her, needed her.

The reality was, he'd never moved on, not really. He shouldn't have left her behind, and that was his biggest fucking mistake. He should have kept her, loved her, showed her who he really was.

"We can't do this," June said, pulling away from him. Her lips were red, puffy, and her nipples were erect, pressing against her bra.

"Why? You want me. I bet you're soaking wet for me, right now. I remember how you'd always want me after I touched you like this." He nibbled her ear, and moved his lips down to suck on the spot right over her pulse. There hadn't been any time to shave, so he had a day's growth on his face, which always served to rub her the right away.

She melted against him, her hands moving around his neck as she gasped. Sliding his fingers up the curve of her back, he found the catch of her bra, and released it. Her tits spilled out. He tossed the offending bra out of the way.

He was rich beyond his wildest dreams, and there had been nothing for him to spend his money on. Now he had a reason, and he intended to devote a great deal of time to his woman and his kid. He had a kid! A son. A little baby boy.

All along he'd had a family right here, and he'd been too stubborn to come and check on her. That had been his biggest mistake.

"You want me, June. You know you do."

"I'll always want you, Killian. I never could stop even when it was wrong."

He closed his eyes, resting his head against hers. "Why is it wrong?"

"Everything I knew about you is a lie, Killian. It's all a lie."

Shaking his head, he held onto her shoulders, and looked into her eyes. "No, it wasn't all a life. That's bullshit, and you fucking know it."

"Everything you told me—"

"The only crap I lied about was all the shit I grew up with. My feelings, who I am, I didn't lie about that."

"You just told me you're a fucking hitman, Killian."

He licked his lips, and took a deep breath. His dick pressed against the front of his pants, and just having her near, it was arousing him.

"I got shot, and everything is all confusing right now."

"Be honest with *me*," he said. "Does my kiss repulse you?"

"No. I just think it's a little early and … too soon to start that right now." She crossed her hands over her chest, and her gaze traveled down the length of him. He was still fully dressed.

Reaching out, he cupped her face, and tilted her head back. "I never stopped thinking about you."

She smiled. "You know, for the longest time I always expected you to come back. I'd stand at the beach, and I'd wait. I'd wonder if that would be the day you'd arrive. I was getting bigger with every single passing month, and then I gave birth. I'd take my son, our son, to the beach, and we'd stand there for hours. I did that for five years until he had to go to school full-time. I never told him why we went to the beach, only that it was important that we were there."

His heart was fucking breaking, thinking about the young woman she had been. How painful it had to have been for her going to the same spot every single day. He didn't even want to imagine.

"So, yes, Killian. Despite everything, just being near you, and I want to jump back into bed with you. I want to feel like that teenager again, falling in love, only now I know I *am* in love. Those feelings never changed, not for me." She grabbed her sweater, and pulled it back over her head, hiding herself once again.

When she put some distance between them, he didn't stop her.

"Would you like something to drink?"

"Do you have any whiskey?" she asked, surprising him.

"I do."

"I could really use a stiff drink right about now. With everything going on, I need something that burns."

"Whiskey coming right up." He moved toward the table in the sitting room. Pouring out two large glasses, he held one out to her, which she took. "Please, take a seat. We've got a lot to discuss."

"You mean seeing as we're not having sex?" she asked, taking a seat across from him. She took a drink, and she frowned as she swallowed. "Wow, that's strong."

"Yep. It's the good stuff." He drank his in one gulp, and poured himself another shot. "It wasn't always about sex with you," he said.

"We don't need to talk about the past."

"We do. *I* do. I know everything about you because you didn't once tell me a lie. I told lies. I fabricated everything to make myself look like the perfect boyfriend. The truth was, the moment that I saw you, I wished I was that person I told you about."

"Killian, you don't have to say that…"

"You know what, I don't give a fuck. It's the truth. You smiled at me, and you were so kind, even with a total stranger. I fell for you fucking hard, and I wanted to be perfect for you. So I told you everything that I wished was true."

There was silence for several seconds. Her gaze fixed on him until finally she broke away and drank more of the whiskey he'd given her. "So what was the truth?" she asked.

"The truth was and is, I don't have a clue who my father is. He could have been a boyfriend, a john, a pimp, anyone."

"A john?"

"I told you my mother was a whore. She sold her body every single night to a string of men. Some were good, most were bad. She gave her body to them, and then a pimp would come and take nearly everything she earned." Even repeating the words now made him sick to his stomach. "I was just a kid, and in her own way, she loved me. All of her friends did. They took care of me, made sure I was loved. I didn't always have food, but I knew that even in their world where children really weren't welcome, they did their best." It was one of the reasons he couldn't stomach hurting women, not then, not now.

It was one of the things that made him weaker than Boss, the owner of Killer of Kings.

"Did you try to find out about your dad?"

"Didn't care who it was, June. No one was worth it. Anyone who could leave my mom like that, in that life, didn't even matter to me."

She stared down at her glass. "Where is your mother?"

"Dead. She died from a final beating from her

pimp."

Her gaze once again returned to his. He saw the question in her eyes.

"You want to ask that question, you're going to need a refill," he said. She hesitated for a split second before holding out her glass.

"I guess I need a refill. What happened after your mother died?"

He poured an even more generous amount of whiskey into her glass. "He had been beating my mom up for years. Using her to amuse himself. Humiliating her to show off to his friends. I was done with him a long time ago, but my mother begged me not to cause too much trouble. Like our son, I was a troublemaker."

She smiled. "I knew he got it from somewhere, and it wasn't me. I really shouldn't be smiling, but I can't help it. Knowing he has attitude and he doesn't take any crap from anyone makes me happy. I don't get to spend all that much time with him anymore, and I want to. I want to so much."

"I know that's what he wants as well."

"He does?" she asked.

"Killian told me. It's why I found him on the beach. He was there, remembering times gone by."

She shook her head. "I'm a terrible mother."

"No, you're not." If there was one thing he'd learned in the few hours of finding her, she was anything but a terrible mother.

"I don't spend any time with him. I can't afford to buy everything he deserves. I'm working so hard. I miss him all the time."

"That's why you're not a terrible mother. You work all the time to put a roof over your heads, food in your stomachs, and you pay the bills, right? That's not a terrible mother. That's someone who cares, who loves.

You're not a terrible person, June. Don't even for a second think that. If anyone's a bad parent, it's your parents for kicking you out. Can't believe that shit. They should be fucking ashamed of themselves."

She glanced back into her glass, and then looked at him. Tears were glistening in her eyes. "I can't believe you're here."

"I'm not going anywhere, June. I'm here to stay. I want to get to know you again, to know Killian, our son. Wow, I can't believe I have a son. He has a thing for spy movies?"

"Yeah, he loves them, and their accents. He's always trying to copy accents. It's cute." She took another sip from the glass.

"I never stopped loving you. I mean that."

"I know you do, Killian. I never stopped loving you either. I just, I can't right now. I don't even know if it makes any sense. I want to, but it has been a matter of hours since you've been in my life. You've hurt people, I've been hurt, and I just need more time."

"I'm not in any rush. I want to prove to you that I'm not here just for that, okay? I want everything."

"You're a hitman. You're going to tell me the truth, I need to know everything. Every little detail."

"Once I tell you, you've got to make a commitment to stay with me."

"Why?" she asked.

"Because everything I do is controlled by a man who takes privacy very seriously, and he's not above killing a woman and child to keep those secrets. I need you to tell me that you'll be mine regardless."

Silence met his words, and it broke his heart to know that she hesitated even though she said she loved him. It wasn't just for Boss's sake, it was for his own. He'd be nothing without her, and just like ten years ago, he was terrified the truth would push her away. He wanted to charm her, to show her they were perfect for each other, not scare her away because there was a hit on her and Killian Junior.

"I won't go anywhere. I'll stay with you, Killian. I promise."

****

Several hours later

The whiskey didn't do anything to numb the pain, not even for a few moments. Killian was a trained killer, a hitman, an assassin. He was trained to take out the enemy, and to make sure there was no trace. All this time she'd been falling in love with a college graduate, he'd been anything but. He'd dropped out of school and fought his way to the top. Impressed by some crazy man known as Boss, he'd become something that she didn't even want to think about. Ten years ago, she couldn't have handled this.

It was a struggle even now.

There was a hit out on her and her son. She couldn't protect Killian Junior from that; only his father could. She didn't like that feeling of helplessness. She was supposed to be the one to protect her son, and yet she couldn't. Killian had told her this was a professional hit.

"I know you're not happy with finding everything out."

She held her hand up, and closed her eyes. "It's fine, Killian. I just need a few moments to process everything. Do you spring this on every woman?"

"There hasn't been anyone else," he said.

June had been staring out of the window whereas now she spun around, and faced him. "What?"

"There's no one else. There never has been. I tried a few months after I left you. I wanted to forget what we had, but kissing another woman made it feel like I was betraying you. There are a lot of things I could do, but betraying you wasn't one of them. You've always been it for me."

"You're telling me that you've never slept with anyone else, never had sex again?"

"Yeah, that's what I'm saying. No one mattered to me, and to be honest, they still don't. You're the only person I want, June." He took her hands, and his thumbs caressed over them, stroking. "What about you?"

"I've been on dates, Killian. I had a son, so I didn't want to know anyone else."

"Killian Junior mentioned something about a cop?"

"Oh, him. He thought he could use Killian's bad behavior as a bargaining chip for dating. It never happened. I guess I had unfinished business with a guy who just left."

He released one of her hands, and cupped her cheek. She gasped at his touch, and closed her eyes. This man was a cold, hardened killer. Someone who couldn't be trusted, but he'd saved her. He loved her, and she knew he wasn't lying.

Looking back, whenever he was telling her lies, Killian couldn't look her in the eye. She had always found it strange, but that was his tell. He couldn't look at her and lie. She didn't know if that was the case for everyone, or just her.

His chin rested on her head, and she wrapped both of her arms around him. She wanted to fall back into his arms, make love, and pretend the last ten years hadn't happened, but she couldn't do it, not yet.

"You're going to need to meet your son," she said.

"I will. He's safe with Bain. He's expecting a kid soon himself. I just wanted some time alone with you.

Believe me, our son will love it there. Scarlett is the mothering sort, and she won't replace you, but he'll have cookies, cakes, and proper homemade food. Everything will be fine. Let me have a couple of days with you. Please." He pressed a kiss to her head. "First I think it's time we get to bed."

"Killian, I don—"

"You're not ready, and I know that. I'm not going to force you, baby. I can wait. I've waited ten years. I can wait some more." He stood, holding her hand to take her toward the bedroom. When she didn't move, he turned toward her. "What's wrong?"

"How did you take care of … your needs if you didn't have a woman?"

He held his hands up. "It's the only thing I could do. I guess this hand is the betrayer," he said.

She couldn't help it when she burst out laughing. "I'm pleased your sense of humor hasn't changed."

"Life is too damn short to spend it not laughing." He pressed a kiss to her lips. "And too short not to do that. One day soon, you're going to be all mine again, June. I'm never going to let you go, not even for a second."

She believed him. He gave her time to take a shower alone, which she was thankful for. She was careful not to get her arm wet. The last thing she wanted to do was to be in any kind of pain. The shot had been lucky, and if she had of flinched or moved, there was a chance it could have gone right through her heart.

Entering the bedroom after her shower, she was surprised so see Killian already in a towel, his hair wet from a shower.

Frowning, she pointed behind her. "I was in the shower. You weren't there."

"I've got two showers, babe. I didn't want to take

the chance of you running off from me." He finished drying his hair, and she couldn't help but admire his impressive, muscular chest. His Celtic ink suited him, decorating those hard, toned arms.

Her cheeks heated, and she turned away from him, not wanting him to see.

"Nothing's changed, June. You used to like looking at me."

"I still do."

Killian pulled her into his arms. "I love you, babe. I'm going to figure this thing out, and then I'm going to spend the rest of my life loving you, raising our kids."

"Kids?"

"Yeah, we're going to have lots more."

She laughed. "You've not even spent all that much time with our son."

"I don't care. I love him no matter what. I'll do whatever it takes to take care of him."

This was what she had hoped. It was like all of her wishes were coming true. Not in exactly the way she wanted them. The last thing she ever anticipated was getting shot, or finding out the man she loved was a killer. Still, right now, she didn't care.

"Come on, let's get some sleep," he said, climbing into the huge bed. "I figured you weren't ready to get naked with me yet, so I left a shirt for you on the chair."

She kept her back to him, for no other reason than she didn't want this to go any further tonight. There was no point in denying that it would happen. She knew there was no way she'd deny him for long. Her body wouldn't allow it. Right now, she just needed to make sense of everything. Besides, she had never been the kind of woman to jump into bed with a guy within the first few hours of meeting.

It had taken Killian a week. A week of spending every waking moment with each other, and even then it was out of character for her. There was just something addictive about Killian.

Once the shirt was on, she threw the towel in the laundry basket, and climbed into bed. The sheets felt like heaven compared to what she could afford.

She didn't argue as Killian pulled her into his arms, and snuggled in close.

"You smell so good," he said.

"It's coconut shampoo."

"I know, but on you it smells even better." He kissed her shoulder. "I love you, June."

"Love you, too."

June didn't for a second think she could sleep, but she did. She drifted off, and slept like a baby.

The scent of coffee woke her up the following morning. Rolling over, she saw it was a little after eight. Getting up, she rushed out of the bedroom, and found Killian standing with a cup of coffee, and a cell phone.

"She's right here, bud. Do you want to talk to her?" Seconds passed, and then he held out the phone. "Our son is on the phone."

There was no time to think as she took the phone, and the coffee. "Hey, honey," she said. Living with Killian Junior for ten years, she was used to being pulled in every direction. Her son had a very lively personality. And having a father could only be a benefit.

"Hey, Mom, this is so awesome. Bain is amazing, Mom. I mean seriously. I didn't know you had friends like this. He's totally wicked, and he's got this video game that lets you shoot people, and Scarlett, his wife, she made the most amazing waffles with syrup. It's great."

"Wow, sweetheart, that's fantastic." She looked

toward Killian who had two thumbs up.

"Yeah, totally awesome. I'm playing this shooting game, and Bain says I'm a natural. I'm like my dad, isn't that great?"

"Erm, that's wonderful, honey."

"Say hi to Dad for me. Got to go. Love you, bye." He hung up, and she was left staring at the phone.

"Our son likes me," said Killian.

"Yeah, I know."

Killian chuckled. "I did good."

"You're sure Bain's okay?"

"Bain's a good guy. I heard the way Killian Junior sounded on the phone. You've got nothing to worry about. Now, I think it's time we had a little talk."

"We talked last night."

"Yeah, this time about our future."

Chapter Six

Killian was on cloud nine. He'd never been so content. After what felt like a lifetime, he had June back, had a son, and everything was going his way.

His cell rang, and June passed it to him.

"Yeah."

"The kid hung up before I could talk to you," said Bain.

"What is it?" It felt odd having civilized conversations with Bain. Only a few months ago, they'd been at odds, ready to kill each other because they were both pissed off with the world. Killian had helped protect Scarlett from Boss, and now Bain was returning the favor by watching out for his son. Friends were always better than enemies, especially since they both worked for Killer of Kings.

"Scarlett found out more details. The head of the Dead Angels MC you knocked off was the father of their current president. He found out you were back in town when you used your credit card at a motel."

He walked out onto the balcony so June wouldn't hear and get upset. When he went on hits, he always paid cash. But the whole trip back in time had been a personal visit, so he didn't think twice about using his credit card in that little shithole of a motel. "Why the hit on June and Killian then? They've never left the town."

"I guess their prez didn't make the connection until they saw you together. Something go down?"

Killian ran a hand through his hair. "I might have killed a few of their men."

"You better talk with Boss," said Bain. "There's more shit, but it's not my place."

June joined him on the balcony just as he hung up. "Everything okay?" She cupped her coffee in both hands. She looked carefree like he'd just felt, and he wished that never had to change.

"I have one more call to make. Why don't you get dressed? Then we can talk." He kissed her forehead, trying his best to hide his concern. Once she closed the glass door, he dialed Boss.

"I thought you were going to get back to me," said Killian.

"I was trying to handle things without you. You said you needed a break."

"You worried about me or you?"

Boss chuckled. "You know I want you back to work, but I was going to leave you alone for a while. The shit is just piling up too deep, and I need it dealt with."

"What shit? Bain said it had something to do with the Dead Angels MC. So what, I just kill their fucking prez again? Not a problem."

"I had Shadow do some recon. They have June's parents, Killian, and they won't give them up until you go in personally."

Fuck. "The parents? Those assholes don't even give a shit about June. They abandoned her when she was pregnant with my damn kid."

"Good. Then fuck 'em. But that contract on June and Killian won't go away by itself."

"Is Shadow still in the town?" asked Killian.

"Yeah. He'll be around if you need back up," said Boss. "There's something I don't understand though."

"What's that?"

"Why the fuck are they after you? Why so personal?"

He knew Boss was questioning his methods. Killer of Kings demanded clean hits, no witnesses, no loose ends. Killian had fucked up that day long ago, but wasn't ready to admit it. As soon as Bain mentioned the

Dead Angels president was the son of the man he'd killed ten years ago, he knew the past was coming back to bite him in the ass. His weakness could now cost him everything.

"Guess they're just assholes," said Killian.

There was silence on the line, and he knew Boss was smarter than that. "I want them gone. Every fucking one. No more mistakes." Then the line went cold.

Killian vaguely remembered that hit from a decade ago. The Dead Angels MC had been dealing in a new kind of drug, allegedly more addictive than crack. It was worse than anything on the streets, and the side effects were extreme. The bodies were piling up, and Boss wanted to end everyone responsible for the designer drug. Boss could have involved himself, demanding a cut of what could have been a lucrative venture, but apparently the old bastard had a heart.

Killian's job had been to get intel on the MC and then take them out so that addictive shit would die along with them. Only he hadn't done his job. Not by Killer of Kings standards.

Now June's family was involved. He shouldn't care because he believed it was karma hard at work, but he knew it would still break June's heart to know her parents were killed—because of him.

Why couldn't he catch a fucking break in life?

He returned inside the condo. June was dressed back in her clothes from the night before, her hair brushed out smooth.

"You look worried. Is everything okay with Killian?" she asked.

He took both her hands. "Of course. Our son's safe, I promised you that."

She narrowed her eyes. "Then what is it?"

"Nothing. Everything's fine, baby."

She tugged her hands away. "You're lying. Again!"

"What?"

"You can't look me in the eyes when you lie. I don't get you, Killian. I promised never to leave, and you still don't trust me enough to be honest."

"It's complicated."

"Do I look fragile? Because if you think I can't handle 'complicated', you've got a lot to learn about me."

He didn't know how to tell her the truth without hurting her. Maybe a white lie would suffice. He'd get his ass back to the town, annihilate every member of the fucking Dead Angels MC, save her parents, and still be back for dinner. Only he couldn't tell her more lies. Her parents would end up filling her in on their ordeal, and she'd hold it against him.

And he'd promised to change his ways.

"I have to go back to town to clean up a few things."

"Why?" she asked, her voice higher.

"I created a problem years ago, and I have to deal with it. Make it go away," he said.

She began to pace in front of him. "Who were you talking to exactly? Was it your boss again?"

He nodded.

"Did you forget all the men with guns, Killian? Did you forget I was shot? I'm not going to lose you! Just forget that town and everyone in it. We'll start fresh, a different place, a new beginning."

June was adorable. She had no idea who she was talking to. Killian was one of Boss's go-to men. He killed without remorse, turning off his humanity to get shit done. And he did his job well. Now that he thought about it, he'd never gone on a hit worried that he might not come out alive. No one was immortal, but Killian trusted his own skill set, from guns and knives to hand-to-hand combat.

"If I don't do this, things will get worse, June. Just let me handle it."

"You said you wanted to talk about our future, right? Well, how can we have a future when there are so many secrets between us?"

He sat down on the sofa, pulling her onto his lap. "I love you, June. More than anything." He held her tight, terrified to lose her. "In my line of work, the number one rule is never to fall in love. My boss always warns us about weaknesses. Love and family are the ultimate Achilles' heel for a hitman."

"What are you saying? You don't want me and Killian? You need to leave us again?"

"Fuck no," he snapped. "I'm saying my enemies look for weaknesses, and when I took you away they went after the next best thing."

She stared at him, waiting for more.

He swallowed hard. "Your parents. They have your parents, but I swear I'll get them back."

"My parents? Why would someone kidnap my parents? I haven't talked to them in years. What does that even mean?"

"It means you need to trust me and let me do my job," he said.

Tears filled her eyes. "I won't put them above you, Killian! Call the police. Tell them what happened."

"This is beyond the police, babe."

"Well, I need you. Killian needs you. There has to be a better way to end all this madness."

He brushed back the hair falling in her face and then wiped her tears with the backs of his fingers. "I started this by shooting those men in the bar. They want payback, and they won't go away until I finish the job."

"You mean kill them?"

Killian stared at her, mesmerized by her natural beauty. Even without a stitch of make-up, she was the most breathtaking thing in the world to him. Her lips were swollen, her eyes glistening with tears. He wanted her happy. He wanted to dream about the future with her, but harsh reality had been thrown in his face.

"You said you accepted me, no matter what," he reminded her.

"What if you get hurt … or killed?"

He smiled and tweaked her nose. "Promise I'll come back."

****

June couldn't believe this was happening to her. She'd just gotten Killian back in her life, ready to plan a future for their little family, and now she could lose him forever.

He'd said to stay in his condo until he came back. She wasn't even sure where his home was located because they'd come in the middle of the night. June did some exploring, trying to keep her mind off the impossibility of the situation. One day she was working nights, a single mom struggling to survive in her simple life. Now she was forced to believe there were hitmen out there living above the law. She'd seen Killian shoot those assholes in the bar without a second thought. He promised her everything she'd dreamed of, but she still couldn't believe a happily ever after was possible for her.

She took a nice hot shower, enjoying the view from the balcony as she dried her hair. After the hours rolled on, she was losing her mind with worry. June stared at the cordless phone sitting on a base in the kitchen. She took a deep breath, then snatched it up and dialed her mother. It was weird calling the number now, after all these years. June almost expected her to answer, but she couldn't. If anything happened to her parents, how would she feel? She'd cut them out of her life once they discarded her. It had been so hard getting started on her own, pregnant and alone in the world. It pissed her off even more that her son didn't have loving grandparents that he deserved. The only good thing out of their cruelty was the fact it made her strong. June could survive, and didn't need a man or a family to rely on.

If she had to choose, she knew she'd choose Killian, but he seemed convinced that he'd always come last in her books.

"Hello?"

June froze. She'd only called out of morbid curiosity, not expecting her mother's voice.

"Mom?"

"June? Is that you?"

She envisioned her mother tied to a chair, a gun at her head. Was the conversation being recorded? Why was she allowed to answer the phone if she'd been kidnapped?

"Are you okay?"

Her mother chuckled. "I'm fine. You'd know that if you ever called."

June's nerves settled. Her mother sounded smug and accusatory, not a woman held against her will. She regretted calling her childhood home. "Where's Dad?"

"He's mowing the lawn. Why?"

"Nobody came to your house? Has anyone been bothering you?"

"June, what's this all about? Are you in trouble again? Should I expect a visit from one of your boyfriends?"

She wanted to scream and smash Killian's phone on the tiled floor. It was like the last ten years never happened, and her mother was still as unsupportive and high and mighty as the day she'd tossed June on the street for being unmarried and pregnant.

"Never mind. Calling was a mistake." She hung up the phone, and leaned against the wall, slowly sinking to the floor. June sat there for the longest time, reflecting on every word her mother had said. She didn't want to care, but it still hurt. The little girl in her longed for acceptance, love, praise. But she was a woman now, with a child of her own.

She took a cleansing breath and picked herself up. At least she wouldn't have to worry about Killian getting hurt. Her parents were fine. He wouldn't have to go in with guns blazing like back in the bar. They could put everything in the past and start over.

Then she thought better. If her parents were fine, then someone just wanted Killian back in town. It was all a set up.

June began to panic. There was no one for her to call because she didn't have any numbers for Killian, his boss, or Bain. She needed someone from the police to make this right, to protect Killian from danger. As much as she hated the thought, she had to call Daniel. He was a cop in her hometown. The asshole had tried to get little Killian sent to juvenile detention so he could date her without the complication of a kid. But she had to put aside her personal feelings for the sake of the man she loved.

She called information and asked for the local police station in her home town. Then she asked for Daniel Fetcher. She gritted her teeth as she waited, hating that she had to sink to this level.

"Daniel, I need your help," she said, not knowing where to start.

"June? Slow down. Tell me what's wrong," he said.

She didn't want Killian to get in trouble. The last thing she needed was to be the one responsible for him getting locked up. How the hell would she explain *that* gem to her son? Daniel was a scumbag, but he's all she had right now.

"I was shot—"

"What? Where are you?"

"I'm okay, but I'm scared the shooter is still in our town. I think he wants to kill Killian's father."

There was silence on the line.

"Where are you, June?"

She began to cry against her will. The stress along with her fears were overwhelming. "I don't know!"

"Hold on, I'll trace the call." There was a long pause. "That's weird. It's untraceable. That can't be right."

"Please, just meet up with me. I don't want anyone else to get hurt."

"Look out the windows and let me know what you see. Find something with an address. Give me something I can use," he said.

She didn't trust him, and didn't want to risk Killian getting hunted down by the police later. In a drawer under the bar she found a handgun and stacks of cash. She stifled a gasp, but instantly knew what she had to do.

"Meet me at the town hall. I'm calling an Uber."

An hour later, she saw his patrol car pull up along the side of the road. "June, get in," said Daniel, after rolling down the passenger window. "Where's your kid?"

"With a friend," she said as she sat down and pulled on her seat belt. "It's Killian who's in trouble."

"Killian?"

"My son and his father have the same name."

He frowned, looking ahead as he turned onto the

main roadway. They sat in awkward silence for most of the drive. This was probably a huge mistake. She didn't like the way he'd once tried to use her son to get a date out of her. There was something off about Daniel, but right now there was no one else to turn to.

As they neared the shoreline, she felt a sense of relief knowing she was closer to Killian. She hoped she wasn't too late to set things straight.

"Where should we start?" she asked.

"'We' aren't starting anywhere," he said. "I'm dropping you off at your apartment and then I'll get to the bottom of this mess."

"Are you sure that's a safe place for me?"

He ignored her question as he stopped in front of her building. "There was a shooting at a bar not far from here. Girls have gone missing. It might be related. Cutting all ties with your ex is probably a smart idea," he said. "You made a good move calling me."

"I thought you were going to help me," she said, reluctantly stepping out. June didn't feel right staying at her apartment. Daniel hadn't asked about her injury, and didn't seemed concerned with her or Killian, just winning her as a prize. She'd gotten to town, and hoped Daniel was actually going to help make sure Killian was safe.

What a mess. This guy was a nightmare, and no way was he interested in making the town safe. He was probably in cahoots with bad people, and now that she was thinking about it, she was only making things worse, but there was no turning back, not now.

She dug in her purse and pulled out her keys. As soon as she pushed open the door to her little apartment, she noticed a huge man sitting at her dinette table. He had a gun in his hand, but he hadn't pointed it at her. Considering the number of tattoos he had, she wondered if he was one of the bikers from the bar coming for revenge. Or was this the same man that had tried to murder her?

"Close the door," he said.

She held her breath, too nervous to talk or make any quick movements. June slowly complied, closing the door, but not taking her eyes off him.

"Who are you?" she whispered. So many thoughts filled her head. What would happen to her son if she were killed?

"You're not supposed to be here." He shifted to pull out his cell phone, resting his gun on the table beside him. "Problem," he said into the phone.

Should she make a break for it? It would take him a minute to grab his gun. She could get out of the apartment and start running, screaming to attract attention. In the end, she chickened out, not ready to take such a risk. One gunshot wound was enough for her.

She hadn't been paying attention to his conversation, too caught up in her own dire thoughts. "I have a son," she said, hoping to appeal to any bit of humanity left in him.

"I know."

At least Killian was in a safe place. It gave her a measure of comfort knowing he was untouchable. The longer she stood there, her legs growing tired, she began to lose hope. This guy probably planned on killing her, so what the hell was he waiting for? As the bleakness of her situation settled in, her bravado increased. What did she have to lose?

"If you hurt me, my boyfriend won't stop hunting you until you're dead," she said. June should be one hundred percent against Killian's lifestyle, but it felt empowering knowing how lethal her man could be. If only he was with her now, protecting her from this beast of a man.

He nodded. "I agree."

She frowned. What was happening? How long was he going to drag this out? "Then it would be smart to let me walk away, right?"

"I'm supposed to keep you here, so no, you won't be walking off." He picked up his gun, released the magazine, and examined it before shoving it back in place.

"Who wants me here? I didn't do anything wrong."

When the door opened behind her, she was ready to collapse. Her nerves were frayed, her body and mind exhausted. She turned around, and found the bluest eyes she'd ever seen.

"Killian!" She threw herself into his arms, holding him close. "I was so scared."

He held her shoulders, holding her back. "What are you doing here? I told you to wait for me."

"My parents weren't kidnapped. It's a trap."

"Yeah, we figured that out." He glared at the guy in the chair. "How did you get here, baby?"

"I took an Uber with some money I found in your condo. I was worried about you."

He cupped her face in his big hands, staring down at her. "God, you're beautiful." Then he kissed her, hard and demanding. She melted against his lips, savoring the sense of love and security he evoked in her. The entire world and its problems went away, leaving just the two of them.

Killian threaded his hands into her hair, trailing his kisses down to her neck. She closed her eyes, tilting her head to give him better access.

When the guy in the chair cleared his throat, they pulled away from each other.

"I'm still sitting here. You want me to leave?"

Killian pulled back and turned to the other man. "Boss gave me an address. We need to end this shit storm before it gets out of hand."

Chapter Seven

The last thing Killian wanted to do was to leave June. She looked petrified, and he was pissed off. The Dead Angels MC had fed the lies to Shadow, hoping to get Killian back in town. Whoever wanted this hit was smart, smart enough to fool Shadow, one of the best. The Dead Angels MC had just underestimated Killian. They'd gotten him back to town, but he was untouchable, keeping under their radar.

"The address can wait, Killian. It's been a long day, and I'd say with how scared she is, you need to go home, and handle shit there first."

"This has to be taken care of."

"Agreed, and I'm not fighting that, but the point of being good at what you do, you take care of your distractions first." Shadow nodded at June. "She's your biggest distraction, and right now, I'm not interested in fighting anyone with your head not fully in the game. I'm not looking forward to being killed anytime soon."

Killian wanted to argue but knew he couldn't. His head wasn't in a good place, and it wouldn't be while he was worrying about June.

"You've got a couple of days. Don't worry about Boss," Shadow said.

"I'm not worried about him." He rubbed at his temples, and didn't see a way around it. "I'll call you soon."

Taking June's hand, he made his way back out to his car.

"What's going on, Killian?" June asked.

"I need to stop this hit on your and our son's head. The only way to do that is to go to the source, and to take them out."

"Kill them?"

"It's the only thing I can do." Ten years ago, he had taken out the leader of the MC, and allowed the old lady and son to live. That had been a mistake, and one he was regretting. "I don't want you to worry about it right now." He took hold of her hand, pressing a kiss to her knuckles. "I also don't want you ever asking that cop for help again. You don't need to rely on anyone but me."

"I was worried about you."

"I know, baby. I know, but I can take care of myself. I've been doing this for years, and I know how to keep myself safe so I need you to do as I ask, and to stay strong." He pulled into the underground garage of his condo, and they made their way up in the elevator. They had privacy now, and he knew he could breathe easily with her safe in his life.

"I was so scared, Killian. You've come back into my life, and it scares me that you're going to leave again. I ... I don't want that for our son."

"I'm not going anywhere." He pressed a kiss to her lips. *So soft and sweet.* "I can promise you that."

"Your promises come really quickly."

"That's because I mean them, every single one of them." He stroked her cheek, and regret filled him. "You have no idea how much I've thought about you the last ten years. You've never not been in my heart, June. God, I wish I could take everything away, and make it all better for you. I fucked up big time."

"Come on. Let's go inside, and I'll make us something to eat. I'm starving." She patted his hand, and he nodded, following her inside his condo.

She still wore the same clothes from a day ago, but that didn't take away from her beauty, from how amazing he thought she was. He watched her for several seconds as she looked into his fridge, and he just couldn't go another second without touching her. Moving up behind her, he wrapped one arm around her while pressing a kiss to her neck. She sighed, and melted against him.

"I don't want to lose you again. I know we keep going over this, and I should probably kick you to the curb, but I can't go through that again. I won't." She spun in his arms, and her hands gripped his shirt. He saw the fear in her eyes and hated being the one that put it in there.

"We're not going to go back. I'm not going to leave. All I have to do is make the world safe for you, and for our son, and we can move on."

"You make it sound so simple." She stared at his chest where her hands lay.

"It is that simple. In my world, there is no way else to look at it. I'm going to fight for you, and for us."

Her gaze returned to him and immediately went to his lips. She licked her own, and his cock thickened. He moved his hand up into her hair, holding her head. "I've got to have one taste of you, June. I can't … I need you." He slammed his lips down on hers, and she didn't fight him.

She kissed him back with a passion that surprised him, but he wasn't going to question it. Sliding his tongue into her open mouth, he pressed her back to the now closed fridge. Her fingers clung to his shoulders, and he took hold of them, pressing them above her head with one of his hands. He ran his free hand down her body, cupping her tit, feeling the hard, puckered nipple against his palm. This was by far better than any of his fantasies. She was perfect, and felt so damn right in his arms.

Breaking from the kiss, he sucked on her neck, loving the sound of her little gasps.

"Please, Killian, I want you."

This had him pulling away, and staring into her

eyes. "You want me?"

"Yes. I want you. Please don't make me wait another moment."

"But you wanted to wait."

"Not anymore."

He wasn't about to question why she had changed her mind. There was no time to take her to his bed. Tearing at her jeans, he had them around her ankles within seconds as he unbuckled his belt and loosened his zipper. Her panties were gone with one hard yank, and he felt more animal than man at this point. Releasing her hands from above her head, he lifted her up, placing the tip of his cock at her entrance. He stared into her eyes, losing himself in her body, thrusting every single inch of his cock inside her.

"Oh, God. Yes!"

She cried out, throwing her head back as he seated himself to the hilt within her. Neither of them moved for a second as he basked in the feel of her pussy tightening around his cock. It had been another lifetime since he'd felt this kind of pleasure. There hadn't been another woman in his life. June had been the only one for him, and that was how it was always going to stay.

Finally, after seconds, minutes, what felt like hours passed, she looked at him, her eyes filled with desire.

"You feel amazing, baby," he said.

"So do you." She licked her dry lips, which had his cock pulsing as a fresh wave of arousal filled him from that one action. She moaned. "It still feels perfect."

He knew what she meant as he felt exactly the same way. Gripping her ass, he held her still, resting his head against her chest. There was no need for them to rush. They had these few precious moments. He knew that reality would soon set in and that he had a time limit.

There was someone out there, determined to take her away, but he wouldn't let it happen, no fucking way. June was his woman, and he was going to protect her. Ten years ago, he had allowed another woman and her son to live. Now those very same people he'd shown mercy to were intent on killing *his* woman and son. He wouldn't let that stand, not now, not ever.

Pulling out of her tight heat, he stared into her eyes as he began to slowly but surely fuck her. This was not how he'd envisioned their first time, but he couldn't hold back. Slamming his cock inside her, he filled her sweet pussy, and moaned with each hard thrust. The fridge wobbled, the bottles inside clattering. She was so wet, so slick—just heaven. Her round curves were even more of a turn-on for him, giving him something to hold on to.

He wanted to see her tits, wanted to drown in them. Tearing open her shirt, he tugged her breasts out of the cups, and groaned as they began to bounce with every single thrust of his cock. Killian loved her big tits. She'd ripened into perfection over the years.

"You're beautiful, June, so beautiful."

"I'm different than you remember."

"To me you're more perfect than ever before." He had to taste her. Damn it, he wanted it all, and as he pulled out of her cunt, sinking to his knees before her, he was intent on having everything.

Lifting her leg up over his shoulder, he teased her clit with his fingers, sliding through her slit, and getting her nice and wet. She whimpered his name, but he wouldn't hear any of it. He replaced his fingers with his tongue, teasing her as he plunged two fingers inside her cunt.

"I've dreamed of this pretty little pussy. Now it's all mine."

He sucked her clit into his mouth, her cream on his tongue, and she tasted divine. He wanted to sample every single inch of her, to come inside her, and fill her, mark her. Fuck it, he wanted her to have more of his children, and surround her with the love that he had failed to do these past ten years. He was going to make up for all of his failings, and show her that there was no one else but him. He was the love of her life, and he wouldn't back down without a fight.

"Oh, that feels so good, Killian," she said.

She thrust her pussy onto his face, and he lapped her up, tasting her, teasing her, driving her wild. He was the only one who would get to do this. There was no one else, not that fucking cop either. Killian didn't like the jealousy that washed over him, but he could deal with the cop, and intended to.

Staring up her body, he watched as she gave herself to him. All of her control was lost in the pleasure of his tongue, and he relished seeing her come apart knowing deep down that he was the only one to do it. She belonged to him in every single way that mattered.

"Come for me," he said. "Come on my fucking face, June. Let me drink you up. I want it all."

She gasped, and it was as if his command set her off.

Her orgasm was strong, hard, and he kept her over the edge, prolonging her pleasure as she screamed his name, over and over again. He wasn't done with her. Killian held her up as he licked at her pussy. Only when he knew she couldn't take anymore did he pull her toward the floor. Spreading her legs, he took hold of his cock, and filled her pussy, feeling her new heat. She was so wet that he had to grit his teeth to control himself. He didn't want to come like a damn teenage boy.

He was an experienced man, but their time apart

made it next to impossible for him to control himself.

Within a few thrusts of his hips, he filled her, his cum spurting deep inside her pussy. He hadn't used a condom, and he hoped that he had given her another child.

Killian wanted to find a means of keeping her close to him at all times.

****

June stared at the white sheets beneath her. She should have told Killian "no", but the truth was, she didn't want to fight his lovemaking, or him, anymore. For ten years she had been so alone with no one to talk to. Her own yearning for him had pushed away any potential boyfriends. She'd even used their son as a means to make people leave her be.

Killian stroked his fingers down her back, and she closed her eyes, basking in his attention. After leaving the kitchen, they had come to bed, and she'd given him time and a chance to look at her body. At first she'd wanted to cover up, but now, she wanted him to see every new curve, and even the stretch marks she had from carrying their son.

"This is where you were always meant to be," he said. "In my bed."

She looked over her shoulder, and watched as his teeth sank into the flesh of her ass, making her giggle. This was a playful side that she'd not seen before, at least for a long time.

The fact still remained that the threat was out there, and she hadn't seen her son in over a day. She missed him.

"What happens tomorrow?" she asked.

Killian paused, and she saw her question had taken him by surprise.

"I know you don't want to talk about this, but it's

important."

"I know it's important." He sighed. "I just wish we had a little more time."

"We do. We have tonight." She took his hand, and pressed a kiss to it. "You'll have me always, but you can't keep me in the dark. You know I've never been good at that. I can't stay here."

"I'm going to take you to Bain's. You're going to adore Scarlett, and of course you'll be safe there."

"Where will you be?"

"I've got to handle this hit, June. I know you're worried about me, but that's what needs to happen."

He moved toward the head of the bed, and he tugged on her arm. She submitted to him, and he positioned her over him. His cock was once again rock hard, and stood tall. Her own pussy was wet, and she slid down his length with ease. She closed her eyes, loving the pleasure of him filling her.

"I'm never going to get bored of feeling that."

"Feeling what?" she asked.

"Your pussy wrapped around my dick. It's so much better than my hand."

This made her smile. Pressing her hands to his chest, she rocked her hips, taking him even deeper, and then pulling up only to slam back down, making them both moan.

"I love you deep inside me."

Killian cupped her hips, holding her in place, and he sat up. "I'll be fine tomorrow. You don't have to worry about me at all."

"What about that man? He didn't look very nice, Killian."

"The men at Killer of Kings aren't paid to be nice, June. They're paid to get a job done, and that's exactly what I'm going to do. I'm going to be getting the job done. Like now." He pulled her down for a kiss, and she gave it to him, cupping his cheek as she did.

She closed her eyes momentarily, enjoying the feel of his cock throbbing inside her. Wrapping her legs around his waist, she felt his much larger, muscular arms hold her. She stared at him, losing herself once again as she had so many times. His blue eyes were a mix of darkness and vulnerability. He was damaged, but so was she. They needed each other.

"I love you," she said.

"You've always been the one for me, babe. Always." He held her tightly, and she rode his cock, needing him more than anything.

They would deal with whatever else they had to deal with, but for now, she just wanted to be loved by him, to remember all the good, and not the bed.

Everything else could wait until tomorrow.

Killian picked her up, and eased out of her. She couldn't believe how easily he moved her about the bed, getting her into position for how he wanted her. He had her on her knees, his cock once again inside her, making her moan, making her ache for him.

"You're all mine, baby." He kissed her neck, sucking on the flesh hard enough that she knew without a doubt that he would leave his mark. She wanted it.

Pushing back against him, she took his big dick, taking him deep inside her.

"Yes, yes," she cried out for more.

He held onto her hips, fucking her hard. He'd leave bruises there as well. Killian made her his, and she loved every second of it.

When he came for a second time, she joined him, and she found a sense of peace. A wave of warm satisfaction flooded her body.

Coming down from the height of their orgasm she

curled up against him, teasing his chest.

The scent of sex was heady in the air. "Will you call me to tell me when you've done your job?"

"You'll know everything. I won't keep anything from you." He kissed the top of her head. She was about to say something else when his cell phone rang.

Killian tensed up, so she knew it was important.

Biting her lip, she watched as he left the bed, his hard ass and massive shoulders a beautiful sight. His back was covered in Celtic tattoos that she wanted to trace with her tongue. He began talking, biting out some words, shaking his head, and then looking exasperated.

"Yes, fine, fine." In the next minute Killian hung up, and moved toward the bed.

"Reality has come," she said.

"Yes, it has."

She took a deep breath. "I better get dressed."

"Hold on." He went to his wardrobe, and came out with a pair of running pants and a shirt. "Scarlett will have something for you to wear, and I'll figure things out for you, but until then, please wear these. Your clothes are not in any shape to wear."

She took them from him, and gritted her teeth. There was nothing else she could do. At least she was going to see her little boy.

"I'm going to fix this, June."

"I know, and I believe you." She looked up at him, and smiled. "I do believe you. It's just hard, you know. I'm used to only relying on myself. I'm having to get used to all the changes, and I will."

June got out of bed, and quickly put the clothes on. She ran her fingers through her hair, and was ready to leave.

"I'm ready to go," she said.

Killian was dressed all in black, and he had a

large black duffel bag. She decided not to ask what was in that, but it looked heavy and bulky. She had a feeling she really wouldn't want to know.

They didn't speak on the journey toward his friend's, at least she hoped it was his friend's place. Everything seemed so surreal. He had a bag of weapons, she just knew it. Less than a week ago she had been concerned about making it to her next job, or how she was going to pay for Killian's new school uniform. They all seemed like worries in the past.

It wasn't long before they were climbing out of the car, and a large man covered in tattoos opened the door. Bain.

"Boss called and said I should be expecting you," Bain said. "Hello, June." He held his hand out.

She hesitated in taking it, afraid that he would crush her, but then she felt silly. His handshake was firm but didn't hurt. Forcing a smile to her lips, she looked between Bain and Killian seeing they needed a minute.

"Can I see my son?" she asked.

"Yes. Scarlett is waiting for you."

Entering his home, she left Bain and Killian to talk.

"Your son has been amazing. He's really good at that video game Bain likes to play. He's passed out for the night I'm afraid."

Scarlett was a nice enough woman, but right now June really needed to see her son. The other woman opened a door, and June stepped inside and paused. There was a small lamp on, and Killian was in bed with a book dropped onto his chest. He looked completely out of it, and in sleep, so damn happy.

A lump formed in her throat. This was the longest she had been without seeing him, and the emotion was threatening to choke her up.

"I'll be in the kitchen," Scarlett said. "He's been so well behaved, June. He's a really good kid."

"I know." There was a chair in the bedroom, and she took a seat, not caring if Scarlett was looking at her or not. This was her little boy. He had changed her life so much. So many people believed that he had ruined her. The few friends she'd had in college had told her to get rid of him, that he was going to destroy her career, and all of her future chances. Tears filled her eyes just thinking about some of their words. Even Daniel had said Killian was a parasite, and that it was her choice to do what she wanted.

When she had felt her stomach begin to grow, and the life inside her do the same, she'd marveled at her own body being able to create life. It was a beautiful thing, and of course it had been her way of keeping Killian's love all to herself.

Even after ten years apart, her love for him was as strong as ever. Killian was going to fight for them, and she had to keep everything together. Even as she was afraid for his safety, she had to believe he knew what he was doing for all of their sakes.

Getting up from her chair, she quietly made her way toward the bed, crouching down to stroke the hair out of her son's eyes.

"He's going to come back for us, Killian, and when he does, everything is going to be different. I won't ever leave you again, I promise you that."

Chapter Eight

Killian drove back to June's town, his music off, mind focused. He couldn't have any mistakes. Those bastards in the Dead Angels MC had known they were being watched. They'd managed to trick Shadow into giving Boss bad intel, hoping to get Killian back in town. He chuckled to himself. Those pricks were going to regret that move. Killian hadn't worked his way up the ranks all these years by being an amateur. He could only be found if he wanted to be.

Now he was going to show up on their doorstep, and he'd show them what a mistake they'd made fucking with his family. There was no way this was professionally done. Something didn't add up about this whole mess. He didn't know exactly what, but he was going to get to the bottom of it.

Although Killian showed pity to women and children, he wasn't a good man. There was a side to him so dark that he kept it locked away, not eager to explore it. When he'd slaughtered his mother's pimp, that darkness aided him, motivated him.

All Boss had to do was give him instructions, and Killian got the fucking job done. It's why he'd moved up the ranks at Killer of Kings over the years. He wouldn't make the same mistakes he had in the past. There was no room for compassion in the killing game.

Tonight wasn't just about money. It was personal.

He called Shadow when he neared the town. "I'll be there within the hour."

"I've got a safe house set up. I'll text the address," said Shadow.

"Let's not fuck this up."

There was a silence on the line. "Are you still blaming me for the bad intel? The Dead Angels knew I was tagging them. I didn't think they were capable of pulling off something like that. Their prez knows what he's doing."

"I've seen what their members look like. I killed a handful of those assholes in a bar—old, drunken, has-beens."

"Doesn't make sense," said Shadow.

"Well, we need to get to the bottom of it tonight. And end them."

"There are a lot of them. The whole town's fuckin' overrun by Dead Angels," said Shadow. "They have property on the outskirts of town, too."

Killian chuckled. "You scared, big boy?"

"Fuck off." The call ended.

By the time he got to town the sun had set, the streetlights creating cones of light along the main strip. He checked the text Shadow had sent him and drove out to the small house near the water. There were no lights on.

Killian stood by his car for a few minutes. With only the moon casting a glow on the ocean, it looked like swaths of velvet. The sound of gentle waves lapping the shore had a calming effect. It reminded him of June.

He knocked on the door, but it swung open as soon as he touched it. The hinges whined, a drawn-out cry revealing a darkened room. Only a few knots in the wood let the moonlight in. Killian reached into his holster and grabbed his Glock.

"Who's scared now?"

Shadow flicked on the lights exposing tabletops covered in select firearms. It was a beautiful display, enough heat to take out the enemy and then some.

"You should really keep that door locked," said Killian, strolling along as he checked out all the weapons.

"Are you joking?" Shadow nodded to the left.

There was a desk set up with a state of the art surveillance system. They'd know if someone crept up on the property before they even thought about it.

"I think that set-up's worth more than this piece of shit shack."

"I'm sure it is. Anyway, Boss's tab, so I'm not worried." There were some maps pinned to the wooden wall boards. With the number of colored markers, Shadow was right, there was a fucking army of Dead Angels and only two of them.

Killian studied the map, trying to plot of the course of action. "Where's the prez staying?"

Shadow pressed a finger to one of the most fortified locations. Killian should have ended that bastard a decade ago. The prez had only been a young teen back then, skinny and terrified. When Killian had to pull the trigger to fulfill his contract, he'd taken away the kid's father. But, even though Killer of Kings demanded it, he couldn't terminate the loose ends, leaving the mother and kid alive after he completed his mission.

His weakness back then had started his clusterfuck, and the time for mercy was over. He planned to fix the error he'd made in the past and then some.

Shadow locked and loaded gun after gun, checking the extra mags were full. "The prez we need to end, why's he alive?"

"What do you mean?"

"Last time you were here, you killed his father, why not him?" asked Shadow, continuing to handle the guns.

"The contract was for the father, not the kid."

This time Shadow turned to face him, sitting on the edge of the table. "Word's all over the street, Killian. The new prez wants revenge for his father's murder. The one he witnessed. Does Boss even know?"

Killian gritted his teeth, his jaw aching as he focused on his next words.

"Look, I wasn't ready to kill a mother and her kid for the sins of the father. I'm not a fucking monster."

There was an awkward silence. Killian knew Boss had been on to him, but he hadn't said anything directly. Why?

"I know about your mother," said Shadow. "Shit, the guys always talk about the carnage you left behind in Ireland."

"That's nobody's business."

"I'm just saying, there's nothing wrong with having pity. You have a soft spot for women and kids, so what?"

He shook his head. "There's no room for pity in our world. I knew better, and now I have to fix it."

"You want to hit their clubhouse?" asked Shadow.

"Not yet. These assholes might be expecting us. They'll be waiting for me without a doubt," said Killian. "Strap on as much as you can carry."

They drove to the end of the main strip, parked, and began to walk. Music radiated out from a few bars. There was a small group of hookers up ahead.

"Hey, handsome," said one of them, reaching for Killian.

"Not interested, sweetheart."

"How about your friend?" she asked.

Shadow's face remained vacant, and he kept walking without acknowledging the women. Come to think of it, as long as Killian had known Shadow he'd never been in a relationship. His named suited him. He was a shadow, a ghost, appearing when Boss needed him at a location. Then he was gone.

When they'd nearly reached one of the rowdiest bars on the strip, Shadow stretched his arm out to the side, bringing Killian to a halt.

"What is it?"

"I guarantee you there are Dead Angels in there. They'll be on call, so we should weed them out before we visit the prez."

Killian nodded. "Let's do this."

Shadow waited outside while Killian went in the front door. They'd only be expecting him. The bar was fuller than he expected, bikers and whores taking their weight in cheap booze. It would be easy to recognize the men he needed to take out by their patches.

No sooner than he walked through the front door, all attention diverted to him. Killian had hoped the music and laughter would mask his appearance, but no such luck in this hick town. Considering he'd killed a few of their members, they'd want revenge.

A couple older men approached him, their graying beards given them a gruff appearance. They reminded him of the assholes who'd hit on June.

"You have a lot of nerve showing up here again," said taller of the two. They were both fully patched Dead Angels, so they needed to die.

"Just came for a drink."

"Bullshit." The man began to circle him, but Killian refused to move. All eyes in the bar were fixed on him, none of them welcoming. Luckily, he was used to dealing with this type of lowlife prick. His childhood was full of them.

"What happened to your face?" said the other man. "Someone teach you a lesson?"

Killian licked his fucked-up lips. No one ever mentioned the deformity, and he tried to forget about it—until he looked in a mirror.

Instead of getting angry, because he was way past feeling sorry for himself, he shrugged. "Actually, yes.

The man who did this to me tried to teach me to mind my business, but I showed him what I was made of when I gutted the bastard."

Killian had only been fourteen. One of his mother's johns got his kicks from beating the shit out of her. Killian pulled the asshole off his mother, and the john held the hunting knife he kept on his belt to Killian's lips. The man demanded an apology for being disturbed. When Killian kept silent thanks to his stubborn Irish pride, the john sliced down through his lips.

Instead of running or crying, the darkness grew, the seed germinating in the fourteen years of bullshit that was supposed to be his childhood. Killian grabbed the knife from the john and plunged it low in his gut, using both hands to slice up through his stomach, disemboweling him. When his mother looked at him from the bed, horror in her eyes, he'd felt a crippling mix of hate and love for the woman.

"I'd like to see you try that on me," said the old man.

"Don't need to," said Killian. "See, I'm not crazy about getting my hands dirty." He opened both sides of his jacket, exposing the custom holster Boss had made for him. It held three handguns on each side, several pockets for extra clips.

"Holy shit!"

The murmurs started, the shock traveling through the crowd like a wave. Some people backed away, some ran or ducked behind tables, others prepared to fight. He noted several guys around his age sitting at the bar, facing them. They didn't appear intimidated or eager to fight, not even setting down their glasses. Right now, Killian had to deal with the immediate threats.

He reached each hand into the opposite holster near his waist, pulling out two guns. From the second he walked into the bar, he'd done a visual sweep, noting the crowd, the threats, the exits, and had begun planning out his first move. He'd give the locals a chance to run, but whoever stuck around was fair game.

"I wanted to leave well enough alone, but since you decided to get personal I have to take care of business." He aimed at the taller man's kneecap and fired off a round. The man screamed and dropped to the ground. "No one messes with my family."

The surge of volatile energy in the bar was fuel to him. He breathed it in as adrenaline spiked through his veins. The darkness he kept under lock and key fought to be unleashed.

Before the second old guy could pull the trigger, Killian shot him between the eyes, and then kept going, killing every man taking an aggressive stance.

The back and forth firing was deafening, the music grinding to a halt. Tables were overturned, women screamed, and glass shattered. By the time he stopped for a breather, the ground was covered in bodies. Some fresh recruits came running in from the back, stopping in their tracks when they witnessed the carnage. Killian was done. He stepped aside when Shadow walked in.

"You were supposed to lure them outside," said Shadow. "This isn't weeding them out."

"It's better this way."

The new heat drew their weapons, one taking a quick shot, the bullet whizzing by Killian's head. Shadow reached to his side and came up with a fully automatic rifle. He positioned it in the crook of his shoulder and rained down hot lead, the men dropping like broken marionettes.

"You think we'll still have the element of surprise?" asked Shadow, stepping over the bodies on his way to the bar. He grabbed a clean shot glass from under the counter and poured himself a hit of whiskey. The entire bar was a write-off, most of the bottles behind the bar in various state of destruction, raining amber. "This is the good stuff." He set the glass back down and ran a hand through his hair.

"There were four guys with cuts sitting at the bar. I didn't get a good look, but they're gone," said Killian.

"They're probably in the body count." Shadow looked around. "The clean-up crew's going to love this."

"No, they're not here. They looked like trouble."

"Were they Dead Angels?"

Killian couldn't see far enough to know their colors, but they sure as hell didn't act like the old-school bikers who'd dropped like flies. They were a next level threat, so maybe there was more to the Dead Angels MC than he'd bargained for. Killian wondered if they were off to warn the prez. "Don't know."

"If they were, they're pussies to leave their members behind for slaughter," said Shadow.

"Whatever. Let's get to our target."

They reloaded and drove out to the prez's house. It would be heavily fortified, no doubt. Killian was expecting something out of a trailer park, not the modern mansion across the street. They parked out of the way and took the rest of the way on foot. This entire hit was surreal, bringing Killian back in time. He still remembered the teenager and woman he'd let live. The kid had stayed crouched behind a small sofa with his mother. Killian had looked them both in the eyes, hesitating when his initial reaction was to end them. A little piece of him was still back in Ireland, a street kid being raised by whores. He didn't want to be one of those assholes who beat him or his mother. In this case, that weakness had led to today.

He'd have to end that kid with the big, dark eyes.

Only he wasn't a kid any longer, but the leader of the Dead Angels MC, eager to claim vengeance for his father's death. Too bad he didn't know what a prick his father was in life.

With the cover of night, Killian and Shadow made their way to the rear entrance. The deep, slow vibration of bass came from somewhere in the structure. And the place was fucking huge. Shadow wasn't able to get a layout of the house, which was unusual.

They were about to turn a corner when Killian felt the cool edge of a blade on his throat. He froze. Normally, he'd fight, deliver an elbow into the enemy's ribs, but this guy knew what he was doing, holding the sharp side so tight to his artery that just breathing put him at risk of bleeding out.

The second Shadow turned and saw what had gone down, he had a gun aimed at the guy's head. Killian hoped Shadow was as good of a shot as he claimed to be. Boss said he was one of his best snipers being ex-military.

"Drop the knife, nice and slow, asshole," said Shadow.

"You're on my turf, so you don't get to make demands."

"Who the hell *are* you?"

"Today I'm known as Manic, but even back then I don't think your friend knew my first name, just my father's."

Fuck! It was him, the Dead Angels MC prez. Why was he alone? Killian had expected an army of security around the leader. He'd gotten exactly what he wanted—his father's murderer at his mercy. Luckily Killian trusted Shadow with his life.

"If you hurt him, you won't walk away with a heartbeat. In fact, I'll be sure to annihilate your entire fucking club," said Shadow.

"I don't want to kill your friend. In fact, he did me a favor ten years ago."

Killian still hadn't seen Manic face to face. He only remembered him as a skinny teenager, cowering with his mother. The guy holding him was comparable to his size, the arm braced over his chest thick with muscle and covered in ink.

"I'm not following," said Shadow.

Manic removed the knife and shoved Killian, standing back into the darker shadows along the side of the house. "My father was a monster. I prayed for him to die long before you took his life."

Killian frowned. None of this made sense. If Manic was thankful for the hit, why was June shot and why was there a hit placed on her and Killian Junior?

"I don't buy it," said Killian. "My mother was murdered. The first thing I did was kill the bastard who did it."

"Then you loved her, but I had no love for my father or the way he ran the club. Now that I'm prez, I want things to be different."

Killian rested his hand on one of his guns. Shadow still had his weapon trained on Manic. "Explain to me why I'm here then. Revenge for killing those losers in the bar? They were messing with my woman. I didn't even know they were part of your club."

Manic laughed. "Don't you get it, Killian? I wanted you here. I wanted you to bring a shit storm of pain to my front door."

****

June couldn't sleep. She tossed and turned, worrying about Killian. He wanted to make things right so they could be a family, but the risks were too great. She still had a hard time believing any of this was possible.

Why couldn't things be simpler?

When the cell Killian had given her vibrated on the night table, she rushed to grab it, her thoughts focused on the man she loved.

"Killian?"

A low chuckle on the other line was deep and menacing.

"Who is this?"

"Your man works for me, June. Right now, I need your help."

She sat up in the bed, her heart racing. Why was Killian's crazy boss calling her? Was Killian hurt or worse?

"What's going on? Is something wrong?" she whispered, not wanting anyone else in the house to hear her.

"When it comes to you, Killian doesn't seem to think straight. He's trying to take on an army with two men. Nothing I say will stop him because he wants the contract on you and your son gone."

"Are you saying he has no chance? Why aren't you doing something?"

"That's why I'm calling you. If I offer you in exchange for the contract, I can get the head of the snake and end all this. Neither of you has to get hurt."

"Why didn't Killian tell me anything?"

He scoffed. "If there's any risk for you, there's no way he'd be on board."

"I'll do whatever it takes to make sure he's safe. I want this nightmare over with," she said.

"That's a good girl. Now, I want you to get ready and be at the front door in exactly twenty minutes. Don't tell anyone. Keep it quiet."

"You're picking me up?"

"No, not me. You've got nineteen minutes." Then the phone went dead.

June put the phone down and rubbed her hands together, trying to bring some warmth to them since her whole body seemed to be going into shock. This wasn't what she'd signed up for, but what choice did she have? Killian's boss said no one would get hurt if she helped him.

She got dressed, tiptoeing around to ensure she didn't wake anyone up. Then she crept down the stairs, cringing when some of the old wooden planks squeaked. When she made it to the foyer, she leaned over, bracing a hand on each knee to calm herself.

"Going somewhere?"

June gasped and spun around. In the dim lighting, Bain looked like the devil himself. How had he heard her?

"I have to do something. Please don't try and stop me."

"Who called you?"

She sighed, not ready to start creating lies. "It was Killian's boss. He has a plan to get Killian back safely. He needs me. I can't screw this up, so I'm going."

Bain exhaled, his eyes narrowed. "He wants you as bait."

"What?"

"Boss doesn't care about you, sweetheart. He just wants to keep one of his top men from dying in a blaze of glory."

"No, he said I'd be able to draw out whoever put a hit on me and my son. Then he'd take care of it and end all this."

"I'm sure that's what he said. I guarantee you, he leaves you on their front doorstep and then fucks off." There was a soft rapping on the door. "Let me guess…"

Bain wrenched open the door, a gun coming seemingly out of nowhere, pointed straight ahead.

"Whoa there, Bain. Just doing a pick-up."

"Not today, you're not, Chains," said Bain.

"Boss's orders."

Bain cocked his gun, apparently not against killing a friend. "Boss wants Killian to come out of this alive, but he's not using his woman to do it. He still has a favor from Viper, tell him to use it."

He slammed the door in Chain's face, and turned around after tucking the gun in the back of his pants.

"I don't want him to get hurt," she whispered, close to tears.

"Killian's good at what he does. He wouldn't have gone if he didn't think he could handle it. Now, Scarlett likes you, and your kid is upstairs sleeping, so I'll let this slide. Don't try and leave this house again. Understand?"

She nodded and trudged back upstairs, occasionally looking over her shoulder. Bain stood at the bottom of the stairs, his arms crossed over his chest. The man was like a centurion, unmoving and intense.

June flopped on the bed without undressing, staring up at the ceiling. She had to have faith that Killian would come back to her. She wanted her son to know his father, for their relationship to grow and thrive. And June needed her man: his love, his presence, his body. She remembered his unique skillset, the way he used his wicked tongue, and the feel of his cock filling her. If he never came back, she'd never want another man.

Her mind wandered in so many directions. What if Boss was right and she'd blown her chance to help Killian? What if two men, no matter how efficient, weren't enough to take on an entire MC?

Chapter Nine

"This makes no fucking sense," Shadow said. "This son of a bitch killed your dad."

"Thanks, Shadow." Killian stared at Manic, impressed with the man he saw today. He was older, wiser, and he clearly had his shit together. When his cell phone started to ring, Killian ignored it, and stared at the new prez. "What the fuck do you want?"

"Ten years ago, you came, and even though your actions helped make my life great, you left a lot of shit behind. My father was rotten to the core. He was a wife beater, a rapist, a murderer. He was everything that made this world an evil place, and he surrounded himself with the same kind of people."

Killian frowned. When he'd been put on the hunt for Manic's father it was because he'd been experimenting in the kind of drugs that hurt a lot of people, women mostly. It kept them sated, but also meant they were sexually responsive so a man could rape them. The drug never made it into production as that had been Killian's job. Boss wanted the drug gone, and the only way to do that was to take out the line that knew about it. He'd done his job, and then left, leaving behind the only woman he'd ever loved along with an unborn child he didn't know about.

"What the fuck do you want from me?" Killian repeated.

"I need your help."

Shadow burst out laughing. "You really think you're going to get his help? You went after his woman and kid."

This had Manic frowning. "I didn't do any of that."

"You didn't put a hit out on my family?" Killian

asked, staring into Manic's eyes. Years of being around scum and he'd learned a thing or two. Manic wasn't lying. He clearly didn't have a clue what was going on.

"I made sure Boss got the intel on the MC. I needed you here. Are you not here because of that?"

"No," Killian said. "Boss has a shitload of explaining to do."

"Agreed," Shadow said.

Killian's cell phone began to ring again.

"I think you should answer that. Whoever it is, isn't going to go away," Manic said.

He didn't want to answer his cell. What he wanted was fucking answers. Pulling out his cell phone he saw Bain was calling.

"Is everything okay?" Killian asked, moving a few steps away.

"Yeah, June and your kid are fine. Boss just tried to lure her out. He got Chains to try and pick her up."

"What the fuck?"

"Something's going on, and I don't like it, Killian. Get to the bottom of this. For now, I've got this place covered, but you need to know something else is playing out, and they're after June."

"Keep them safe." He hung up his cell, and looked toward Manic. "Okay, let's get this straight, you need and want my help."

"That's right."

"Why?"

"You only took out a couple of the MC ten years ago. My father's poison has spread like a cancer. Now there are some people who want this way of life. Who want to..." Manic stopped, and looked away. The shame on his face was clear.

"What is it?"

"I need you to kill the bastards that followed my

father. I've got a list ready, but I need you. You're a hardened killer, and right now I need someone who can kill without asking questions."

Shadow sighed. "Why now?"

Killian looked toward Shadow. "Does it matter?"

"Yeah, it matters. You killed this little prick's dad ten years ago, and now he magically asks for your help? He knows you're a killer, and you're going to go wandering into the lion's den, and be shocked that you got fucking bit. You don't go in all guns a blazing. You don't get shit done like that."

"Worked just fine, I think," Killian said.

"Why?" Shadow asked, pointing a gun at Manic's forehead. "I have no problem killing you. In fact, it would give me a great deal of pleasure because I'm bored. When I'm bored, I like to kill people and make beautiful art with their blood."

Killian had to give it to Manic, the guy didn't bat an eye.

"You want the truth? There are a group of us that want the MC on the straight and narrow. We're all about the bikes, the life, the cause. I want to make a fucking difference. I don't want kids to be afraid. How can I make a difference when three weeks ago, my father's buddies took two teenage girls, chained them to a table, and did a train on them?"

"A train?" Killian asked. He wasn't exactly well-versed in lingo.

"Each member took a turn," Shadow said. "One after the other. Was it consensual?"

Manic shook his head. "No. What I found out was that they wanted to amuse themselves and put the town in place, they took two random girls. They weren't even fucking eighteen years old. They didn't want it. What I walked into, that shit is fucked up. I took them to the hospital, and I got word that both girls killed themselves. My club was responsible for that shit. There's a cancer within us, and I need to get rid of it. I have to stop it one way or the other. You're my only hope. You think I'm a pussy for caring, I don't give a fuck. Ten years ago I watched you, I saw how you killed my father. You didn't even fucking blink, and then you walked away. That's what I need, and I will pay whatever fucking price you need, but I have to take them out."

"Will you be joining in the fun?" Killian asked.

"Yes. I'm club prez, and I've made sure that my men are ready for this. We all want them fuckers to pay for what they did, and what they've done." Manic ran a hand down his face. "One of the girls was a brother's sister's friend. She wasn't family but close. While I was taking her to the hospital, she asked him why he didn't save her. That shit, it's got to stop. I know how to stop it."

Killian held his hand up. He didn't need to hear anymore, and was done listening to this shit. "I need to know who put the hit on my woman and my kid. He's ten years old, and I've got them safe for now. I want answers."

"I didn't put any fucking hit on any kid or woman. I've got standards, man. I don't do that kind of shit."

"Someone did. Someone close to you."

"I can find out. It could be one of the guys checking in on my old man's killer."

"Then you find out, and you call us. Until then, I'm not helping you with shit."

Killian didn't wait around. He left with Shadow close at his back.

"I've got something to take care of."

"Why do I feel you're about to do something

really stupid?" Shadow asked.

"Because I am." He stopped as Shadow grabbed his arm.

"You've got to rethink everything you're about to do."

"What I'm about to do is deal with the bastard who thinks he can harm what's mine. No one, and I mean no one, uses my woman as bait."

"You're going after Boss?"

Killian didn't say anything. He was so fucking pissed. He wanted to hurt everyone and everything. After ten years of being a loyal fucking dog to that bastard, and the first time his back was turned, he went to the only woman he had ever loved, and intended to use her as fucking bait. That shit didn't sit well with him.

There was a pit of rage that needed to get out, and the only person who was going to satisfy him right now was Boss. From the moment he began working for Boss all those years ago, he'd known deep down in his heart that the fucker was a cruel man. He'd even been convinced that the bastard didn't have a heart, and he was right. There was nothing in Boss. All that man cared about was his bottom fucking line.

"Look, I get that you're pissed right now, and I do understand, but there are bigger fish right now."

"I know Manic needs our help, but until he tells me exactly who's responsible for sending hitmen after my woman and kid, then I'm not playing."

"Those old club members are bad news for a lot of people."

"I know. And I don't give a shit. Now, unless you want to end up on the dead pile, you'll get out of my fucking way. I want blood, and I want it now, and you're the only person standing in my way."

There was no fear in Shadow's eyes, but Killian

didn't expect it. Every single man and woman that was associated with Killer of Kings, had lost that part of themselves years ago. None of them had feeling, or remorse, or even love. The only time he'd seen it in Viper or Bain recently was when they were with their women.

"You're making a mistake."

"Don't care." He shoved Shadow off, and kept on walking.

"Do you even know where Boss is?"

"I know where that fucker is." He'd been working for him for longer than he'd not been working for him. Heading toward the now closed pier as it was late, he climbed the gate, and dropped down on the other side. Glancing toward the security cameras he saw they weren't in operation, which was a guarantee to him that Boss was here. Wherever the owner of Killer of Kings went, nothing and no one followed him unless he wanted it.

His hands were shaking he was so wired, so ready to kill, and he wanted to. He made his way toward the peak of the pier, and paused when he felt a presence behind him.

"Looking for someone?" asked Boss.

Killian whirled around. "What the fuck do you think you're using my woman for, huh? You think that shit is funny?"

There was no laughter in Boss's eyes. "Are you quite finished?" Boss asked.

"You tried to take her away from me."

"I did nothing of the sort."

"You sent Chains. Your little lapdog driver. Don't fucking lie." He was past any rational thought and grabbed his Glock, pointing it at Boss's neck.

"I'd think twice about pulling that trigger."

"Why? Because you've got that revenge hit on

anyone who kills you? You think I give a shit? I've spent my entire fucking life looking over my back. You think I won't be prepared to take out every single asshole who comes after me for taking a hit out on you?" He spat the words at him, wanting Boss to know exactly how he felt.

Still, Boss didn't show any signs of fear or anger, or even remorse. There was nothing there. His eyes were empty. "What about June and Killian Junior? Are you going to let them live the rest of their lives constantly looking over their shoulders? Neither of them deserves that."

"Do not bring them into this. Do not bring them fucking into this!" He yelled the words, feeling the raw pain more than ever before. He was a father to a ten-year-old kid. There was no way he was ever going to be able to allow him to go through any more shit, not from him. It was unfair, and he wouldn't do it, he couldn't.

He didn't lower the Glock immediately. There were moments like this that he wished he had Boss's balls of steel.

He had a son and a woman to take care of now. There was no way he could risk killing Boss, and spending the rest of his life constantly being hunted down. Slowly, he stepped away, and glared at Boss. "Are you going to attack me? Put me in my place for daring to mess with the king?"

"I'm not a king, Killian. I never claimed to be one. I kill those that need to be brought down, but I'm not one of them."

"You were going to use my woman." All the adrenaline was beginning to fade away.

"Yes, because I know what the fuck I'm doing. I was going to use her to bring out the person who started that hit," said Boss.

"What do you mean?"

"There's some twisted shit going down in the Dead Angels MC. That club needs purification."

"But Manic said it wasn't him."

"It wasn't, as otherwise I'd have called you to end him. The kid is trying to do shit right, and I can't fault him for that."

Killian paced, rubbing at his temple. "Then who?"

Boss held his hands up. "Enough with the questions. Just understand that I was trying to save your woman and kid. They would never have been in danger. They would have had protection, Killian."

"June's been through enough. No more. I won't have her hurting because of me. Whatever you need to find, you come to me and only me."

"Fine, but it's going to take longer."

"I don't care. I really don't fucking care right now." He stepped away. "I've got to go to her."

"Then go, Killian."

He turned away from Boss and left, surprised that the man he worked for didn't try to stab him in the back.

****

When the bed dipped beside June, she jumped out, gasping. She held her hands into fists, ready to hurt anyone who came near her.

"It's me, baby. It's me," Killian said.

"Killian?"

"Yes. It's me. There's no one else around. It's just me."

"Thank God!" She jumped on the bed, and threw her arms around his neck. "I thought you were dead. I thought that something bad had happened to you because I didn't get to go to Boss."

The moment he touched her, she moaned in a good way. Ten years without his touch, and she was desperate to feel his hands on her.

"Nothing can happen to you," she said. "Do you hear me? Nothing."

"I won't let anything happen to me, baby. I promise. I love you so much." He breathed her in, and she closed her eyes.

"Does Bain know you're here?"

"Yeah, he nearly shot one of my nuts off. He's so damn bad at times."

"Don't try to make a joke. I can't handle a joke right now."

"Hey." He cupped her chin. "Everything is going to be okay. I promise." He pressed a kiss to her lips, and she felt like she was drowning. Her pussy was on fire, and she craved his touch more than her next breath.

When she made to push him to the bed, Killian took control, and pressed her against the mattress. He moved between her thighs, and she gasped. His cock was hard as he thrust it against her core.

"I just wanted to hold you."

"I want you to make love to me, Killian. Please." She tugged on his shirt, and as he began to take clothes off her body, she did the same with him, needing his bare skin next to hers.

When they were both naked, Killian kissed her once again, only this time he didn't linger on her lips. He kissed to her neck, then to breasts, sucking one nipple and then the other. She arched up as the sensation of his lips on her tits went straight to her clit.

"Your body is fucking beautiful, baby. So beautiful."

Down his lips went, stroking over her stomach before going to her mound. He held her legs spread, and then his tongue slid between her slit. He stroked her clit, gliding down to plunge inside her.

He held the lips of her pussy open, and when she

glanced down, he was staring up at her.

"You taste so good."

"Oh, wow, you feel amazing," she said. "You're so good at this."

"I could live between your legs."

When he thrust his tongue again inside her, she cried out. It felt great, but she needed his big cock so much more. They had been apart for too long, and they were making up for lost time. Their feelings for each other were the same, but now it was more, deeper. She had no idea she could feel this way about anyone, especially not for Killian.

"I love you, baby," he said. "I want you to come on my tongue."

She fisted the blankets beneath her, and as he circled her clit, stroking over the highly sensitive bud, she couldn't control her orgasm, or prolong it. She hurtled straight to that beautiful place of raw bliss, crying out his name, and giving him everything he ever wanted.

The pleasure rushed through her body, leaving her panting.

Before she had finished, Killian moved over her. She saw him quickly roll on a rubber, and then he was inside her—deep and hard. He took hold of her hands, pressing them above her head as he slammed every inch of his dick to the hilt.

They both groaned.

"You're all mine. All fucking mine."

She held onto his hands, intertwining their fingers, not wanting to let go. From the first moment she'd seen him, she'd belonged to him. No one else would ever do. There was no way she would ever have been with anyone else because deep in her heart, she'd known all along that Killian was the only man she was ever going to love. Going with anyone else would have been a betrayal to herself.

In the back of her mind, she had always been hopeful that he would come back, and he did. It was surreal.

"Love you, baby. Fucking love you so much."

He began to fuck her, pulling out, only to push back inside, going deeper still.

"You were born to belong to me," he said.

"Yes. I'm yours, Killian. Always." She wrapped her hands around his neck, kissing him, tasting herself on his lips.

He held her down as he thrust inside her. Lifting her hips up to meet every single thrust, she stared into his eyes, knowing she'd do anything for him, risk her very life to make sure he survived.

When he rolled over so that she was on top of him, she smiled down with a giggle. His hands went to her hips as she began to rock on his cock. He was so big, filling every inch of her and then some.

"Let me see you come apart, sweetheart. Touch your clit for me."

"You want me to do naughty things for you?" she asked, teasing him.

"Yeah, I do, and I can feel how much you want to do them." His hands tightened on her hips, which made her moan.

Rocking on his cock, she decided to give him a bit of a shot. Cupping her tits, she teased her nipples, feeling his cock pulse inside her.

Down she went, running her hands over her body. Finally, she got to her pussy, and teased a finger through her slit, finding her clit.

Staring into his eyes, she played with her pussy, bringing herself closer and closer to another orgasm.

"That's a pretty sight," he said. "So damn pretty.

Come for me, June. I want you to do it all over my cock."

His hands moved up her body to cup her breasts, and then down to her hips. She loved the way he gripped them, and seemed to know exactly what he was doing with her body.

"Please, Killian. I'm so close."

"I'm not going to fuck you until you give me what I want."

She teased her clit, and as the peak began to happen, she came, screaming his name, wanting him more than anything else as the orgasm overwhelmed her. Killian changed position, pushing her to the bed. He held her hips as he rode her, thrusting deep inside her cunt, taking control as she came all over his cock. When she pulled her fingers from between them, he placed them in his mouth, sucking on the tips.

"You taste amazing," he said.

"Come for me now," she said.

He did. Killian held her to the bed, and began to fuck inside her, riding her hard. Throughout it all she held him close, feeling and seeing his pleasure was something she loved to watch.

She had him just as he had her.

Afterward, he didn't pull out of her, and they lay together, staring into each other's eyes.

"I missed you today," he said.

"I did you as well. I miss you all the time that you're not here. Does that make me sound like a crazy person?"

"Not at all."

The smile on his lips faded.

"It's not over, is it?" she asked.

"Not yet. The threat is still out there, and while it is, I need you and our boy to be here."

This was the hard-hitting reality for her. What if

he didn't make it home?

"Don't go. We could go anywhere, Killian."

"I won't run from this, June. I can't. That's no life for you or for Killian. I can fix this."

"But what if something happens? What if I'm left all alone again? I don't think I can do it."

"You won't have to. I've put provisions in place. You won't have to wor—"

She slapped his chest. "Do you really think this is about the money? I don't give a fuck about the money, Killian. I want you, not some damn dollars. You."

He smiled and that only made her frown. "Baby, you're the only person in my entire life who has ever just wanted me, and it makes me love you even more for it."

She kissed him again, needing him to know that for her, it was always about him, not anything else.

Chapter Ten

Killian had always lived life in the fast lane, never stopping to reflect. When he was young, it had been about survival, and then it had been about forgetting everything that had fucked with his head. He'd never expected to have a family, because he'd never really had one growing up. Killian loved his mother, but she'd been a lost cause, and he spent most of his time on the streets. He'd learned how to steal, to fight, to charm, and later, to kill. There were no other options. When he excelled in his life of crime, he never looked back.

Now that June and Killian were in his life, he was ready to become everything he never had. It wouldn't be easy, but it would be worth it. He wanted to be a good husband and father, to embrace that love he'd first felt with June ten years ago.

First things first. Killian needed to help Boss tear down the Dead Angels MC. He wasn't afraid to kill, and he was damn good at what he did.

He stopped at a hotel along the highway to get some sleep. There was no way he could get any rest with June in his arms, and it would be harder to walk away in the morning. She was too much of a temptation. Just thinking about her gave him a boner. He couldn't believe how lucky he was to have her as his woman. And not just any woman, but the mother of his son.

After a decent night's sleep, he showered, changed, and hit the road. By the time he pulled into town it was ten in the morning. He wasn't worried about the element of surprise, not when Manic had practically begged him to kill his own fucking crew. He wasn't sure if it was an act of valor or the worst kind of mutiny, but it wasn't his club to worry about. Manic wanted the old-school bastards dead and gone. They were lazy, disobedient to the new prez, and lacked the basic decency that even stone-cold killers managed to hang on to.

Killian didn't have a problem with prostitution. His own mother had been a whore, but he didn't agree when under-aged girls were forced into it. Manic's new members weren't saints, far from it. They were still hardcore criminals, but at least they had some standards. Even Boss knew where to draw the line.

Killian picked up his cell and called Shadow. "I'm back in town. Did Manic give you anything we can use?"

"He has no fucking clue," said Shadow.

Killian exhaled his irritation. All the time he'd been away and they were nowhere closer to finding the source of the problem. "Then what? We start handling Manic's problem? Maybe one of them will name drop with a gun to their head."

"Boss is sending backup. I think he knows more than he's letting on."

Killian squeezed the steering wheel as he drove, trying to contain the fire he felt growing inside him. Didn't Boss trust him to handle the job? It pissed him off that he'd sent more backup. Killian didn't need a babysitter. He'd made one fucking mistake when he'd killed the original prez, leaving witnesses, but there had been ten years of clean hits since then. Didn't that amount to anything in Boss's books? And why the secrets? After all these years, he'd hoped Boss trusted him with sensitive intel. Maybe pulling a gun on Boss was a fucked-up mistake he'd live to regret.

"Who's he sending?"

"He didn't say," said Shadow.

"Let's just get this shit done. If I have to end every one of them, including Manic, so be it."

They met at the safe house near the water.

Shadow walked out to meet him at the car. "Have you eaten?"

"I can't think about food right now," said Killian.

"Well, I'm fucking starved. Let's get a bite to eat before business."

Killian ran a hand through his hair, too tired to argue. He supposed it would be smart to be at their best. Killing worked up an appetite.

Shadow got in the passenger seat, and they drove into town. It wasn't exactly smart showing their faces around town after the bloodbath last night, but Killian never was one to cower in fear.

There was an all-day breakfast diner close by, so they went in and took a table by the window, facing each other so they could watch each other's back. Some things were unconscious in their line of work.

"Can I get you boys something?" asked the waitress, pulling a pen from behind her ear, poising it over her worn pad of paper. The place was a dive, a greasy-spoon if ever he saw one. Killian was used to the best. Ever since getting hired on at Killer of Kings when he'd moved over from Ireland, he'd enjoyed the high life. But he wasn't an asshole, and remembered where he came from every day of his life.

"Give us a minute, sweetheart," said Killian, still busy scanning the interior. He hated this town, and not just because of all the bullshit since he showed up, but because it reminded him of losing June and finding out he'd missed out on so many years of his son's life. When this was all over, he wanted to stay as far away as possible, start fresh with the woman he loved.

"Cop," said Shadow.

Killian looked over his shoulder and watched the lone cop walking the beat along the sidewalk. It didn't surprise him to see an extra police presence. There was nothing out of the ordinary, until the cop stopped dead in his tracks looking Killian straight in the eyes.

Shadow cleared his throat. None of them liked cops. They didn't meld with their lifestyle.

"Relax," Killian whispered.

The cop entered the diner, the bells clanging against the glass. Why was he staring at him? Killian played with the saltshaker, twirling it one way then the other, not taking his eyes off the cop.

"Killian, right?"

The officer pulled an empty chair from another table, the legs scraping along the tile, and sat down at the side of their two-person table. As soon as Killian heard his name, his hackles rose.

"I don't remember ever seeing you before," he answered.

"Well, I'd recognize you anywhere. You're the spitting image of your kid."

He braced himself to stand up, but Shadow kicked him from under the table. Killian ground his teeth together and sat back down.

"You know my son?"

"I think the whole police department does," he said before chuckling. Killian wanted to punch him right in the face. "But then again, I'm more concerned about you."

"Yeah?"

"A few days ago I picked up your ex from the town hall. She was worried about you, thought you were in trouble again."

"Again?" asked Killian.

So this was the bastard who had his eyes on June, and wanted his son out of the way. He gave the other man the once over, not feeling emasculated in the least. Killian would be able to take him down bare-handed in ten seconds flat. What he didn't like was a history he wasn't sure of since he wasn't around. Had anything happened between the cop and June?

The cop had a cocky smirk that Killian wanted to wipe off. "She's been single for a reason, right?"

He couldn't bite his tongue another minute, even though he knew he should. They were in town for a reason, and this asshole was just a distraction he should avoid.

"You know nothing about our relationship, so I'm really not sure why we're having this conversation."

"What relationship? You don't think she'd take you back after all these years, do you?"

"Already happened, Huckleberry Finn," said Killian. "In fact, I was busy fucking her all night long."

"*Oh shit*," Shadow muttered, leaning back in his chair.

Killian was never one to follow rules or respect authority. There'd only been a couple times in the past twenty years that he'd been hauled into jail, but he'd always been out within the hour thanks to Boss. No charges. Besides, this cop was way out of line.

"You wouldn't know anything about the shooting last night, would you?"

"What shooting?" asked Killian.

The cop nodded, his eyes narrowed. Did he want to fuck June? She was Killian's, and he didn't plan on handing her over.

"June's not at her apartment."

"And how the fuck would you know that?" asked Killian.

"Someone had to look out for her all these *long, lonely* years."

This wise-ass needed the shit beat out of him. "Well, I'm back, and I'm not going anywhere." He raised his hand in the air to get the waitress's attention. Another minute with this asshole and he'd put a bullet between his eyes. "We're about to order, so if you don't mind…"

The officer stood up, adjusted his hat and palmed his service revolver as some kind of pitiful threat. Killian had a .357 Magnum in the back of his pants and an arsenal in his trunk. Shadow was always well strapped, and Killian knew that bastard would have his back.

"Good to meet you. I'll be seeing you around." The cop sauntered out of the diner, looking back a few times as he disappeared up the street.

"Are you insane?" asked Shadow. "We're supposed to be on the down low. When shit starts going down again, that cop will have you in mind for the charges."

Killian scoffed. "I'm untraceable, same as you. Besides, I don't get caught, and I sure as hell ain't worried about that hick cop." Every hitman to sign up with Killer of Kings was wiped clean and had their fingerprints removed. Killian wasn't worried about being called out for a crime. He was busy planning how he'd fuck him up for playing games with his woman. He needed to show him, police officer or not, that she was his property and Killian didn't share.

They finished up their breakfast in silence. Killian's head was elsewhere. The fact the person who'd put out the hit was still out there didn't sit well with him. He needed to talk with Manic and find out if he'd had any luck rooting out the problem. They drove out to the mansion on the outskirts of town, walking up to the front door this time. Before they even pushed the damn doorbell, they were flanked by four of Manic's men.

"Why the fuck are you ready for trouble this early in the morning?" asked Killian.

"You showed up, didn't you?" asked the one with

the short beard and facial tattoo.

Killian put his palm over his heart. "Do I look like fucking trouble? I'm just here to see a friend."

The front door opened, and Manic stood in the entryway wearing just a pair of grey joggers. "It's okay, Rebel. I was expecting them."

The men gave them the once over and then left them alone with their prez. He invited them inside, and Killian reluctantly entered. This wasn't a social call, as he just wanted information.

"I'll admit, I wasn't expecting you to show up here," said Manic. He walked over to a black leather bar with granite top and poured himself a hit of hard liquor, knocking it back.

"It's not even noon," said Killian.

"Considering I haven't been to bed yet, this is the only thing keeping my head on straight," he said. "You get the job done?"

"Look, asshole, you're not my boss, and I'm not being paid to work for you. These hits are coming from the goodness of my heart."

"Relax, big boy," said Manic, running a hand through his hair. He looked like he hadn't slept in a week.

Killian walked around the room while Shadow stayed rooted in place by the door, a hand inside his jacket at the ready. "Did you have any luck finding out which member of your club called for the hit?"

"Right to business, eh?" Manic sat on one of the stools. "The call came from here. From inside my house. Your Boss traced the number and reamed me out a few hours ago. He knows more than me."

"We'll have to go through all your members. We have ways of getting men to talk," said Killian. "Those old bastards are probably still sleeping off their hangovers, so it's a good time to make it happen."

"There's more," said Manic. "A few more teens were taken yesterday. Their parents reported them missing. Young blonde girls, same description as the last two that were kidnapped."

"You think it's the same members of your club?"

Manic poured another glass. "Just do what you're good at and end those assholes. All of them. Find the girls and you'll probably find your man."

Shadow opened the front door, so Killian didn't stay and argue. They drove out to one of the bigger compounds owned by the club and cut the engine.

"This'll be fun," said Shadow.

"Two of us against an army isn't my kind of fun. Not anymore anyway. I need to come out of this shit alive."

"That's always the idea." Shadow double checked all his clips and then got out of the car. The air was already warming up, the sound of birds creating a deceptively tranquil setting. Things were about to get ugly.

As they approached the one-story structure, a gunshot rang off inside, then another, forcing both of them to draw their weapons. They passed the rows of Harleys lined up and kept their backs to the side wall of the brick building.

"Wouldn't that be nice, the assholes killing themselves off before we show up."

"It's never that simple," said Killian.

The front door burst open, and a teenage girl ran out. Killian holstered his weapons and grabbed her around the waist, pulling her to the shadowed side of the building. When she attempted to scream, he slapped his free hand over her mouth. "Hush," he said.

One of the bikers came out a few seconds later, looking around for the girl. Shadow came up behind him, a gun pressed to his neck. "Don't move, motherfucker."

Once they were all safely hidden from the entrance, Shadow pistol whipped the biker.

"I want to know who put a hit on my woman and kid," said Killian. "Be smart and answer if you want to live."

"I know who you are. You won't let me live anyway, so I'm not saying shit."

Killian sighed, scratching his head with the barrel of his gun. "Wrong answer."

He turned his attention to the girl for now. "What happened in there?"

"They said we had to work for them, to sell our bodies. If we refused, they'd kill us." She started crying. "She's crazy. You have to help my friends."

Killian looked over at Shadow, his eyes narrowed as he tried to piece this together. He wasn't expecting to hear about a woman being involved. As far as he knew there were no women in positions of power in the Dead Angels, so this didn't make sense.

"Keep them here," said Killian. "I'm going in."

****

June left the kitchen after lunch. Her son was still eating and watching cartoons on the flat screen television on the wall. She could hear Bain and Scarlett in the small office off the hallway. They were talking about Killian and not being able to find out what they needed. She even heard Bain say that Boss was probably right about using June to lure out whoever wanted them dead.

No matter what he thought, Killian couldn't fix this on his own. June was no shrinking violet in need of sheltering. She'd fought every day of her life as a single mom. Assholes hit on her every shift at work, but she dealt with it. June didn't need saving. Now she had a son to think about, one with a hit on his head, and a man she loved that seemed to have a death wish.

She went upstairs to her bedroom and called Boss.
"Hello, June."

"I need to take you up on that offer," she said. "Can you get me out of this house without Bain trying to stop me?"

Boss chuckled. "I sent Chains with no such luck. Bain's taken your safety personally, so there's no way I'll be able to get you out without his consent. Besides, Killian doesn't want you involved."

She exhaled, feeling cornered and frustrated.

"There's something I have in mind. I'll be in touch." The call ended.

Not ten minutes passed, when there was a knock on her bedroom door.

"Come in," she said.

Scarlett slipped inside, closing the door behind her. She had some clothing in her arms. "We look about the same size. I thought you could use something different to wear."

"Thank you."

She sat on the bed beside June, resting a hand on her back. "Bain wanted me to talk to you," she said. "We know you want to help Killian, and that's fine. I totally understand that. Bain didn't want you doing anything that could get you hurt, but if you still want to help—"

"God, yes! Please let me help him if I can."

"The only way Bain agreed to let you go was if Boss took you personally. That says a lot because he rarely gets involved himself. He knows who put the hit on you, and he'll end it. Boss is a hard ass, but I trust him. I even work for him."

"And my son?"

"We'll keep him here. Keep him safe," said Scarlett. "And don't worry, Boss won't let anything happen to you. I know that much."

She nodded, not trusting herself to speak when so many emotions were on her sleeve. June wasn't used to people being kind or helpful to her, and she certainly wasn't used to fighting for love. Killian was all she had. After briefly talking with her mother recently, it had only solidified the fact she had no one else in the world besides her two men.

Half an hour later, there was a knock on the door. June was wearing the cutest floral summer dress thanks to Scarlett. She'd used her time to prepare herself emotionally for what was to come. And she wanted to look beautiful for Killian.

"Chains," said Bain. "Boss better be in that fucking car or she's not leaving my house."

"He's there. Relax."

"Nothing happens to Killian's woman," he said, a very clear threat in his tone. "Remember what he left behind in Ireland? That'll be us."

She watched from a bottom step of the staircase as Chains opened his jacket to expose an array of lethal weapons. "I've got this, Bain. It ain't my first rodeo."

By the time she got to the vehicle, her nerves were heightened. She'd only heard bits and pieces about the owner of Killer of Kings but never met the notorious bad boy.

"Take a seat," Boss said after Chains opened the rear door for her.

She got in beside him, a full seat separating them, which she was thankful for. The car began to drive away from the house, and she wondered what she'd got herself into. Killian would be furious that she agreed to this.

"Are you sure this is safe?" she asked.

Boss shifted slightly in his seat. His eyes were dark and evil, his long black hair still damp from a shower, loosely brushed back.

"I promised Killian nothing would happen to you, and I always keep my promises."

She swallowed hard, feeling intimidated in this man's presence.

"Who would want to hurt me?"

"Someone who wants to use you to get to Killian. It's not who I'd expected, but I plan to end them today," he said. "I don't like being blindsided. In all fairness though, I found this particularly interesting. I think it'll work to teach Killian a lesson."

He spoke in riddles to her.

"And then what?"

What did she expect to hear? Did she want him to admit that he would kill another person? He ran his hand over a series of simple bracelets on his right wrist. They were thin leather bands with tiny black beads, a few of them colored.

He noticed her looking. "It's a personal tally," he said. "Of kills."

"Hits by Killer of Kings?"

Boss shook his head. "My kills. This year."

Her mouth felt dry and scratchy. She didn't say another word for the rest of the trip.

They were getting closer to home, her old home. When this was all over with, she wanted to settle somewhere far away from old memories.

Boss pulled out his cell and made a brief call. "Put the word out that June Harris is in town, staying at the Loreli Motel. I want two million for a live exchange."

June gasped. "You said—"

He put a finger to his lips. "Don't question my methods."

His cell rang. "What's going down?"

She strained to hear what the other man on the

line was saying, but she couldn't hear anything more than garbled voices.

"Shit. This isn't even our fight. Tell Manic to get his sorry ass down there. I'm not the fucking Dead Angel's bitch."

He told Chains to change directions.

"What's going on?" she whispered.

He chuckled. The man showed no fear, only annoyance. "I wanted the party to come to us, but it looks like it's already started."

Chapter Eleven

Killian moved down the long corridor and the club seemed to open up. There were lights, and he saw some cameras set up as well. If this was going live, he was royally fucked, but something told him it wasn't. The entire room had been set up like some kind of studio.

"Well, well, well, I never thought I would live to see you again."

A bright light shone in his face, and he put his hand up, trying to protect himself from the sudden glare of it all. The person who had spoken was clearly a woman. Killian held his gun out in front of him. Shadow was outside, and right now this wasn't sitting well with him. Killian knew he needed to be on the top of his game, as otherwise shit was about to go down, and he didn't like that.

Don't screw this up.

For some reason, in that moment, he seemed to think about a time many years ago before he'd even met June when he was having a conversation with Boss.

"I can't kill women!"

"I get that you think they're weaker than us, but I want you to realize that they have a strength that no one ever expects."

Killian laughed. "You're fucking daft. Off your rocker. Women don't deserve to be hurt."

Boss sighed. "One day you're going to have to make a choice, to kill or not to kill. You need to be sure you make the right decision."

Over the years, Killian had thought about that one conversation. He'd always believed that killing women was for weaker men. Boss had killed women, and a part of Killian had always hated that about him. In a way, he felt Boss was too cynical when it came to women.

"I see that I'm confusing you. I've always found that about men. I guess in a way, it's why I've enjoyed dangling precious little fruits in front of them."

The bright light was hurting his eyes, and he was struggling to look ahead. He couldn't see anything as weird shapes appeared in his vision.

Suddenly, he was grabbed, and as he tried to pull out of the hold, his gun was shoved away from him. He reached behind him, and pulled out his knife. Stabbing blindly in front of him, he heard the grunt, and he kicked his leg out.

Out of nowhere there were about six men all over him. His arms were grabbed, the knife was wrenched out of his hand, and he was held down.

"Have you finally secured him?" the woman asked.

Killian fought as he was lifted and pressed against the wall, chains secured around his arms. He tugged on them, but they wouldn't budge.

"Very nice. I have to say he's even better looking now than I remember."

"What do we do if Manic shows up?"

"Tell him that his mother will be waiting for him back at the house, and if he doesn't complete the shopping, she'll have a meltdown."

Killian looked around the room, seeing several old bikers, and they all moved out of the way, giving him a clear shot of a beautiful woman. She had to be in her fifties, maybe even older, but it didn't look it.

"Ah, I see you don't remember me. I guess a lot has changed over the years."

She was wearing a tight-fitting dress that molded to her hourglass figure. Her hair cascaded over one shoulder, and he just knew that this was the woman he'd let live.

Manic's mother.

Through the fog of his mind, he believed her name was Lauren.

"Ah, I can see that little cloud is clearing."

He glared at her, and only her. "What the fuck do you want?"

She walked up to him, slapping him around the face. It stung, but he was used to pain.

"That is no way to speak to a lady of any kind." She tutted. "Didn't your mother ever teach you any manners?"

"My mother was a whore," he said.

"Well, I guess your son is going to grow up with the same problem that you did."

He tensed up at the mention of his boy.

"When I first got the word that you'd breezed back into town, I didn't believe it. I mean, who would have the balls to come back to a town that he left after killing someone?

Then I find out that the same man who took my husband from me, has a woman and a child himself. It was just too good to let go."

Killian watched as she grabbed a chair and moved a little closer to him. He saw several of the MC were at her back, and clearly didn't know what to do. They were waiting for her command.

She had her own little army.

"Do you like what you see?"

It was then that he took in the rest of the room. In the far corner there was a bed, and what he saw had him sick to his stomach. Three ugly-assed looking blokes were screwing a young girl at the same time. Even across the room he saw the fear, the pain, and also sorrow in her gaze. Tears streaked down her face, and Killian couldn't believe that a woman could allow this to happen in her presence.

Lauren followed his gaze, and sighed. "A wonderful sight if you ask me. I always did like to see men break them in while they're young."

Killian returned his gaze to her. "You allow this?"

"I set it all up. I was the one that was investing in that precious little drug. It would have made us a fortune, and believe me when I say I get off on this."

Suddenly, Lauren stood, and walked over to the bed. Even as the girl was being raped by three men, she cowered away from the woman as she touched her. Manic's mother was truly evil. There was no doubt about it.

"You took so much away from me. When you came to kill my husband, I did believe you were coming for me, but then I realized that there was something off about you. Never did know who you were, but I got a sense from you that even though you were a monster, much like myself and my husband, you had an issue with morals. You see, darling, when you have morals, you tend to make mistakes."

It was killing a part of Killian's soul to see what was happening to that girl.

"You'd be surprised how much people would pay to see this kind of stuff. A man sees what he wants, and he takes it without any questions asked."

He was going to kill this bitch. Suddenly, he understood now what Boss was trying to tell him. A monster could take any shape or form. It didn't have to be a man, but could just be a woman as well.

All of his life he'd taken pride in not killing women, and now watching this bitch in front of him, he wondered how many other girls had died because he'd let her live.

He wanted to get to the very core of this sickness

and exterminate it.

"Does your son know what you're capable of?"

Lauren threw her head back and laughed. "My son doesn't have a clue about anything. He's all about a new order, a modern way of running the club." She spat on the floor. "I sometimes have to wonder if I gave birth to him, and his precious ways. He thinks he can take over the club. He doesn't have a clue what the fuck is going on."

Killian was shocked to see the disgust on her face at the mention of her son.

"It's going to be easy to take them out though. Men like my son die every single day, and I was happy to let him live, but now it's becoming a bore to see the guilt in his eyes. He's no son of mine, and a huge disappointment."

She took another seat on the chair, and stared at him. "With you though, I'm thinking a more fitting punishment is due. Your wife, she's on the fat side, but that just means we can hurt her a little more. I love it when they scream and beg."

He clenched his hands, and she cackled.

"Wow, you really do love that little slut, don't you?"

He didn't say anything. His rage was building and as he stared at the woman, every single belief he had now began to shatter around him. She was going to die, and he was going to make sure that he put the bullet between her eyes.

"You think I don't know what you're thinking about right now? You're thinking about what you're going to do, aren't you? You want to hurt me, to make me pay for hurting those girls. You men, you're all the same, thinking you're some kind of hero when it's the furthest thing from what you are." She stood up, and placed her hand on his chest.

Just her touch sickened him, but he stared into her cold eyes.

"You think you're going to get away with this?" he asked, knowing that if he died right now, Shadow or even Boss would make sure this bitch didn't live to see another day. He wanted that. All that he hoped was that he'd get the chance to see her fall.

She chuckled. "I've been getting away with it for as long as I can remember. You think this is my first rodeo, killer? I know what I've been doing because I've been doing it all my life." She stepped close, and her lips were pressed against his ear. "If you must know, my first victim was my sister. She was so sweet, so delicate, and by the time they were finished with her, I made sure she was only a shell of her former self. I've been with my husband all my life, and we're two parts of the same whole." She pulled back. "I've been in this game a lot longer than you. I know what I'm doing, and I'm skilled enough to make the right men turn the other way." She pressed a kiss to his cheek, and he pulled back. This only made her laugh even more. "Your disgust is pathetic. I've been doing this for a long time, and I've yet to be caught. There are a lot of people who like what we do, and do you really think you're going to stop them? You couldn't even figure out who put the hit out on your woman." She pressed her hands together and smiled. "Some men do like fat women, and I just know she's going to make us a fortune, and then I'm going to get that little boy to eat out of the palm of my hand." She ran a hand down her body. "I've heard that young boys like a woman who knows what she's doing."

Killian was going to gut the bitch, and fuck her up so much that she didn't even know what the fuck the problem was.

"First though, I think it's only fair that my boys have a little go at you." She pouted and stroked his cheek. "I'm sorry about this because you really do have a beautiful face, even if it does have some scars on it. You and I both know that they make us stronger."

Killian watched her saunter off as three old fuckers stepped forward. Metal covered their fingers, and he smirked. "You really think I'm afraid of you fuckers. It's a shame that you let a dirty cunt tell you what to do."

It was a surprise to see Lauren insulted by his words. She was a disgusting human being, and when he got free he was going to make sure that she couldn't breathe.

The first hit went to his stomach, but he was used to harder punches. He'd taken them as a kid, and growing up. Part of his training to be part of Killer of Kings was proving he could take the torture without giving away vital information. He'd been young, but Boss had been thorough with his methods.

Gritting his teeth, he glared at her, knowing that Boss had a plan. The owner of Killer of Kings always had a plan. All he had to do was wait it out, and hopefully, at the end of it, he was going to be breathing. He had so many plans after all of this. First, he was going to marry June, and take her away from all of this bullshit. He was going to make sure that his son wanted for nothing.

All of this would come to pass. He would make up for the past ten years. He just had to get through this.

****

"What the fuck are you doing here, Shadow, and where's Killian?"

June looked over Boss's shoulder, but she didn't get a clear shot of the man. She was terrified as they were not at the hotel. During the journey in the car, she had gotten the sense that something had gone really wrong.

Tension was thick in the air.

Boss had been on the phone, talking so fast that she didn't have a clue what was being said.

"He went in, and I just got out. It's the wife," Shadow said. "The wife put out the hit on Killian's woman and kid. Also, you're not going to like this."

What June heard next was enough to turn her stomach.

"I had no idea," said another guy with lots of ink and a leather cut on his back.

"You're telling me this woman you call a fucking mother has been taking girls and exploiting them and you didn't know? She used them in a sick and twisted fuck game, and you're saying that you didn't have a clue what the hell was going on?" Boss asked.

She heard the anger in his voice, and it made her feel cold inside. Boss was clearly a monster, but the way he was talking, he had standards.

"I didn't know. She never said a fucking thing, and it's not like she'd turn around and tell me that she got off on seeing girls raped and tortured." The leather-clad man paced up and down. "Fuck, fuck, fuck."

"You've got one choice to make as far as I'm concerned. She dies, and all the fuckers that are related to it die along with her," Boss said.

"Boss, the website is fucking huge," Shadow said. He was on his cell phone. "Maurice said there's an entire network at play."

"Then we do what we do best, we bring the kings down. I won't have that website up any longer than it needs to. You tell Maurice there's a healthy paycheck if he gets that website down and all the addresses related to that sick shit. Daddy's going to have a party." Boss climbed into the car, and then several of the leather-clad men joined them.

June sat in the corner, not knowing what to do. She was afraid, but Boss was staring out of the window. No one spoke for the longest time and then Shadow got in the car.

"We going to get Killian now?" Shadow asked.

"Of course we are." Boss looked at her. "How do you feel about acting?"

"I can do whatever it takes. If it will help Killian, and anyone else, I'll do it. What do you need me to do?"

"You don't need to know the plan in advance. I've got a feeling it will be even more authentic if you just react." Boss stared at the biker who was next to her. "Are you prepared to do what needs to be done, Manic?"

"You're asking me to kill my mother?" he asked.

"I'm asking you to deal with the poison that is infecting your club. You think this is going to go away, or do you think she's going to allow you to live much longer? You've got to get your head out of the clouds, boy. Don't forget that women can be just as vicious as us."

Boss sat back, and June stared out of the window.

Time passed, and it was too soon before they were out of the car. She gasped as Boss grabbed her around the neck and pointed a gun at her head. This was all a little too real, too raw, too damn scary. She was petrified of what was about to happen.

This was for her son, for Killian, and for all of the other girls that had been hurt. She had to do this for them, and to hope that no other girl found her death in the clubhouse up ahead.

Scarlett had promised that she would take care of her son, no matter what, and June believed the kind woman.

Entering the clubhouse, Boss pointed the gun at another leather-clad man.

"I've got something your lady wants, and tell her I'm not letting this bitch go without a fight." Boss growled each word, and he didn't lower his weapon.

She held onto his arm, trying to deal with everything that was going on. It was scary, and she hated it. June had never been as afraid in all of her life as she was right now. She knew something was about to go bad.

Closing her eyes, she waited, and tried to drown everything else out. Suddenly they were moving forward, and there were shouts, grunts, cries. They entered a much larger room, and seeing what was going on in front of her, nearly had her throwing up all over the place.

"So this is his little slut," a much older woman said, coming forward.

Past her shoulder, June gasped as she caught sight of Killian being beaten against the wall.

"I take it you're Lauren," Boss said.

"The one and only. Who might you be, handsome?"

"I don't give names," he said.

"Don't worry. I can handle no names." Lauren reached out and stroked June's cheek. "She looks so sweet, so innocent, so tempting. I know a lot of men are going to love getting their fill of you."

June squeezed Boss's arm tighter. She couldn't help it. The fear was too much, and it scared her.

What was the plan? What did Boss hope to achieve?

There was no easy way out of this, not that she could see. There was only pain and death.

"It's quite the little set up you've got going here. You bring all the girls here, make them do what you want?" Boss asked.

"It's all for their own good. Yes, this is the perfect place, and we're able to market it worldwide. We have a huge fan base."

From the way Lauren looked at Boss, she liked what she saw. There was no way that Boss was going to be suckered in by all this. The rage she heard from him was not something you made up.

"Maybe one day you could stay and watch the show."

"I don't rape girls!" Boss moved the gun from June's head, and fired his gun at the two men at her back. "And I don't let bitches like you near me." Boss shot her in the arm, and Lauren lurched back before steadying herself.

June was shoved to the ground as Manic and his crew rushed into the room. Bullets were flying everywhere, and June saw that Killian was still trapped to the wall. She had to do something before he got hit in the crossfire. June crawled toward Killian trying to stay as low as she could, when someone wrestled on top of her.

"You think you're so smart right now, slut. Wait until I have the entire club lining up to take your pussy. I'll have them tear it apart, and then I'll cut you piece by fucking piece." Lauren slammed June's head against the floor, dazing her for a little bit.

Fear, panic, or adrenaline—she didn't know what it was—but she was able to shove Lauren off her back, and slap her hard. When Lauren attempted to get up, June pulled her arm back, clenched her fingers tight, and punched her in the face.

Lauren went down, and that was when June saw the keys hooked at her waist. After grabbing them, she ran over to Killian.

"You shouldn't be here," he said. "You're supposed to be safe with Bain."

"Shut up, because right now, I'm the one helping you." She found the key, turned the lock, and as a series of bullets ran across the wall, near where they were standing, Killian pushed her to the floor.

"I've got to fucking end this once and for all," Killian said, kissing her cheek. "I love you, baby."

He kissed her head a final time, and it was then that she realized the noise had gone silent.

Killian helped her to her feet, and that was when she saw the men who'd been in the car, were in control. Guns trained on most of the older men. Manic was there, staring at his mother. Her nose was bleeding, and June got a sick sense of pleasure at seeing the blood running down her face.

"You did this?" Manic said. "My own mother."

"Please, give me a break. You're such a fucking pussy." Lauren got to her feet. Blood coated her arm in crimson.

"Remember what I told you," Boss said. "This is your problem to deal with. I'm getting fucking tired of cleaning up everyone else's mess. Clean this shit up!"

Killian held her hand tightly, and she watched as Manic's hand didn't shake. "I know what I have to do."

"Then do it already."

Boss wasn't helping the situation. Killian squeezed her hand, and then she watched as he left her side. He went to Manic, patted his shoulder, grabbed the gun from him, and shot Lauren in the head.

"No one should ever have to kill their own mother, no one."

Chapter Twelve

Killian watched the bitch fall to the ground, and a rush of raw satisfaction washed through him. He stood transfixed as blood pooled on the concrete around her, a morbid canvas.

She was the first woman he'd killed.

He remembered life as a young boy, hating how men treated the women who'd raised him. Whores or not, they didn't deserve what those assholes dished out. Killian had promised himself never to become that kind of lowlife. In this case, an exception was in order.

"Damn, that was a long time coming," said Boss. "You're the rightful heir to the Dead Angels, Manic. I hope you'll handle your shit better than your mother."

"I'm nothing like her," said Manic. He shook his head, looking down at the body. Even if the woman was a fucking monster, it couldn't be easy for a kid to see his mother's dead body. Killian knew first hand. At least Manic didn't have to pull the trigger.

"You okay?" asked Killian.

"Yeah. It had to be done," said Manic. "It's just hard to believe I have no family left."

Killian realized he'd personally taken both this kid's parents from him. He knew what it was like to have no one and nothing, only himself to rely on. It had made him hard. Made him invincible. He hoped Manic would be able to forgive him one day.

"You have your club. That means everything. Patched for life, eh?"

Manic nodded absently, still staring at the body.

Viper came up behind Boss, resting a hand on his shoulder as he took in the scene. "You've got three IOUs, and this is what you want me to deal with? Fuck."

"Anyone loyal to the dead bitch needs to join her.

Take Shadow and Manic and hunt down anyone outside the club. It only takes one piece of shit to spread the disease, so end it. No mistakes. I'll have the clean-up crew in town within the hour," said Boss. "By the way, you'll be paying for it, Manic. This is your shitstorm, not mine."

"Whatever, I'm not worried about money, just deal with it," said Manic.

Killian put his arm around June and held her close. The pungent, abrasive scent of gunfire lingered in the air. Manic's crew was already rounding up the old bikers, handling them execution style. The two remaining girls were already gone, probably to the hospital. It was over. No more worrying about June and Killian, no more putting off his dreams of a forever family.

"I won't lecture you," said Boss. They faced off for a minute, and Killian could hear every unspoken word from just the eye-contact. Killian had fucked up. He'd been weak, left loose ends ten years ago, and didn't take Boss's advice. The list went on, but there was no way Killian would be put in this position again. It was a hard lesson learned.

"Did you know all along?" asked Killian.

Boss smirked, not saying a word. He didn't have to. The bastard was always one step ahead of everyone. The thing with Boss, he had patience, and he liked some lessons to be learned rather than taught.

As much as he wanted to leave town, Killian still had to hang around to help Killer of Kings. There was more than just a body count to clean up. Manic's life had been turned upside down, and part of Killian took personal responsibility for Manic since he'd let him live all those years ago. He couldn't be older than twenty-five, but he was strong and weathered. Growing up in an MC was no cake walk.

First things first, Killian needed his woman. With all the chaos and stress, he had to unwind, to drown in June's sweetness. He kissed her temple, then whispered in her ear. "You look beautiful in that dress. Lose your panties. We'll be leaving in a few minutes."

He walked over to Shadow, pulling him aside. There were still occasional gunshots deeper in the club, shouting, and cursing. The place was being torn apart by Manic's crew and Boss's men. "I just want to thank you for hanging around and having my back," said Killian. "I know you were hired for recon, so I appreciate it."

"It's what I do." Shadow ran a hand through his hair, looking around at a crumbling empire. "Maybe we'll work together again one day. You're Boss's little bitch, so I'm sure I'll see you around."

"Fuck off." He gave Shadow a playful shove. "You heading home after this?"

Shadow nodded.

Killian didn't know anything about Shadow, but most of the men working for Killer of Kings liked their privacy for one reason or another. "You have family?"

Shadow scoffed. "Don't have one of those." He jutted his chin towards June. "Looks like you just got the whole package deal."

Killian couldn't help but smile. "Yeah. I have to learn how to be a dad. No practice run. Hopefully I don't fuck it up."

"You'll do good," he said. "You can't do worse than that bitch."

Killian looked at the body one last time, still shocked that a woman could be so evil. Boss had been right, and Killian was glad she was dead. Soon she'd be gone, any twisted legacy buried with her.

As he started to leave, Manic called out to him. "I just wanted to say thank you."

He met up with the other man. "I killed your mother, you don't have to thank me for that."

Manic shook his head. "You let me live a decade ago, and you didn't have to. Boss asked me to pull the trigger, and you spared me. That deserves thanks in my books."

He felt a unique closeness to Manic, what he perceived as a parental bond. Instead of making an enemy, he'd made a friend, a new connection. "If you want to thank me, give me the keys to one of those bikes. I need to clear my head before dealing with this shit storm."

"After today, half of those Harleys won't have a rider. Take your pick. Keys are always with the bikes."

They parted ways for now. Killer of Kings would be in town for a few days to sort shit out. Boss would want to lay down the law so the Dead Angels MC knew who not to fuck with. Killian would need to be by his side. At least there was an end in sight.

"Come on, baby." Killian took June's hand, and they left the club, emerging into the clean air outside. The sky was blue, the tree line offering a sharp contrast of color. No matter how hard life hit him, Killian always fought back, looking for hope and beauty in the smallest things.

When they reached the bikes, Killian motioned for June to get on the first one.

"What? I'm not getting on that," she said.

"Yes, you are, little lady." He held the handlebar and forced her to back up into the side of the bike, his body pressed to hers. "Did you do as I say?"

She looked up at him, questioning.

"I told you I wanted the panties gone."

June smiled. "I wasn't wearing any."

Killian groaned, reaching under her dress to

ensure she was telling the truth. He ran the backs of his fingers over the soft hairs of her pussy, before plunging in two fingers to the knuckles.

She gasped and grabbed his shoulders, her eyes fluttering closed.

"You like that? Now get your cute little ass on that bike so we can get the fuck out of here." He nipped her earlobe. "You're going to ride my dick, long and hard."

June turned and attempted to get on the back of the bike. He helped lift her into the seat, before sitting comfortably in the front. It had been a long time since he'd ridden a bike, but he used to love it in the summers. He started up the engine and revved it a few times to get the feel of it before hitting the gas. The power and vibration under the seat were incomparable. He left the club and hit the road, needing to get anywhere private fast. His cock was uncomfortably stiff in his jeans, and June's arms wrapped around his waist weren't helping his predicament.

He drove over the rolling, paved roads in the outskirts of town, until they reached a crest that overlooked the water. Killian pulled over and stopped, bracing both feet on the ground. The ocean seemed to go on forever, miles of open space. He imagined it leading all the way to his homeland, but there was nothing for him there. Or here. The only place he wanted to be was with June and Killian.

"It's beautiful, isn't it?" said June. "I love the water. I could sit here all day." Her breath was warm against his neck. God, he loved her so much.

"Where you need to be is sitting on my cock." He palmed the front of his jeans and then began to unbuckle his thick leather belt. It was a relief when he unzipped and gave himself more room.

"At the side of the road? On a motorcycle?"

"I need you, baby. Let me make you feel good." No cars had passed, but even if one drove by, he didn't care.

June cautiously climbed off the back of the bike, and Killian shifted back a bit and helped June put her legs around him. Once they were face to face, her thighs spread wide, her dress immediately rode up to her hips. Her pretty pink pussy glistened in the sunshine. He wet his lips, wishing he had time to do down on her, but he had a lifetime to get between her legs and explore her body. She'd changed so much over the years, maturing into the most lush and tempting woman he'd ever seen. He'd spend the rest of his life making love to her

Right now was about fucking.

She looked down at his bulging boxer briefs.

"You like it? Do you like my cock, June?"

She nodded, running her fingers over the length.

"It's all yours, baby. Anytime you need to be fucked, that's what I'm here for," said Killian. And he was always ready. Just thinking about June had him raring to go.

He pulled his boxers out of the way, his cock jutting out, hard and virile. She bit her lower lip and began stroking him, up and down. Killian closed his eyes and savored her touch.

"How can you think about sex now?" she asked. "I'm still shaken up from everything that happened. This isn't the life I'm used to."

"And you won't be getting used to it. From here on out, smooth sailing, baby girl."

"Promise?"

"No matter what happens, I'll always be there for you and Killian. You're my life, and I was a fool to think I could walk away the first time," said Killian.

She slipped the straps of her sundress and bra down her shoulders, allowing those huge tits to spill out. They were fucking delicious, and he'd never get enough of June's body.

"That's my girl." He grabbed her waist, pulling her forward until his face was buried between her tits. Killian sucked on her pebbled nipples, drowning in that perfect softness. Pre-cum slipped from the head of his dick. She was driving him crazy.

June moaned, the tension in her body easing away. "God, that feels good."

"Put your feet on the pegs and sit on my dick. I'm hard for you, June. You're all I think about."

She did as told, bracing her weight up on the pegs as she held onto his shoulders. He fluffed up her dress as she positioned herself over his erection. Killian closed his eyes as she sank down, her tight cunt grabbing his dick.

"Fuck, you're perfect." He groaned when she was fully seated, holding her hips in a bruising grip. "Ride me hard, baby. Show me how much you love fucking your man."

****

June liked the sound of that. She wanted to be Killian's—body, soul, and mind. She was afire with need. Just one look or touch of Killian and she was gone. No regular man would do for her. She was a big girl and needed a strong, capable man to handle her. Killian was raw strength and power, his charm and confidence off the charts. He held her securely while keeping the bike in place, and she never once felt unsafe in his arms.

His shoulders were broad and hard with muscle. He was so beautiful and deadly rolled into one, his ice-blue eyes piercing in the sunlight. His thick, hard cock filled every inch of her, satisfying her in ways only he could. She might complain, but she loved his no holds barred attitude and dirty side. They complemented each other perfectly.

When she began to rise up and down, the pressure immediately started to build deep in her cunt. She watched his eyes roll back as he licked his lips. His beautiful lips. June leaned forward to kiss him. She wanted all of him.

"I'm sorry for all the bullshit I put you through," he said between kisses.

She cut him off by kissing him deeper, their tongues mingling. He tasted like spearmint. The entire world went away, leaving just the two of them. His kisses moved to her neck as he held her waist on either side, lifting her up and down over his cock. He took control, using his strong arms to help her ride him.

A lone car drove by, but she was past caring that they could be seen fucking on a motorcycle. She could smell the ocean, hear the waves in the distance, and Killian was ravishing her body.

"Such a dirty girl," he said, taking her harder. "You're all mine. Mine to fuck. Mine to keep."

"Yes," she said. "Make me yours."

His fingers dug into her hips as he pistoned in and out of her with increased intensity. She felt so full, so completely claimed. As her orgasm surfaced she couldn't help but cry out with each exhale. He rocked her body in just the right way, taking her into that beautiful pre-orgasmic bliss. When her body finally erupted, she wrapped her arms around Killian's neck and held on as the erotic waves hit her hard. He growled and rammed her hips down over his cock a few more times until he filled her with his hot cum.

They held each other until their breathing settled, the warm breeze cooling their heated flesh.

"Sorry, sweetheart. I couldn't wait until we got

home. Next time, I'll take you nice and slow." He combed his hand through her hair, and kissed her once on the lips. "You can't even imagine all the things I want to do to your gorgeous body."

June was speechless, and turned on all over again. He was still inside her body, their connection more intimate now that the urgency of their desire had settled.

"Where is home?" she whispered.

"Not here, I know that for sure," he said. "You and Killian love the ocean, eh?"

She nodded. "It doesn't matter though. I just want somewhere safe, somewhere we can put down roots as a family."

"I want that, too," said Killian. "I'm going to talk to Viper. Boss had me help find him a waterfront place a while back. You might like that town."

June couldn't imagine raising Killian in an urban condo, so she was open to other ideas. All she cared about was getting settled so she could focus on being a good mother.

"I don't care where we go, Killian. Every town has restaurants and bars. I'll be able to find new work."

He scoffed. "Are you fucking kidding me, babe? From this day on, you're my woman, and that means you'll be taken care of. You deserve the world, and I'm going to give it to you—and our son."

"I hope our son will be okay with all the changes," she said. It felt weird, but good, to say "our son" because she'd always been a single mother with the weight of the world on her shoulders. It would be nice to have a partner to raise Killian, but also to give her the love and security she desperately craved.

He helped her off the bike, and then he zipped up and joined her. "Come here," he said, taking her hand.

They walked to the edge of the cliff, and June

backed up when they got too close.

"It's okay, I've got you." He pulled her into his embrace and held her close, pressing her cheek to his chest as he kissed the top of her head. "And I'm never letting go."

Then he bent down on one knee, holding her hips in his hands.

"What are you doing?" she asked.

"I never had a father, so I'm not sure what the fuck I'm supposed to do. No one tossed me a ball or helped with my homework. All I can do is promise you I'll do my best, every single day."

"You'll be a great father, Killian, I know it."

He smirked. "I'm not afraid of anything. Never have been. But I'm scared to death of doing this wrong."

"We'll do it together."

He cupped her ass and rubbed his face against her swollen mound. "And you. I know exactly how to take care of you, beauty." Then he took her hands and kissed them. "I'm going to love you and take of you exactly how a man should. How *I* should have."

Killian reached into his back pocket and pulled out a small brown leather pouch. He fiddled with it, finally revealing a Celtic designed gold ring and a huge princess cut diamond.

She stared in awe, not even making a connection to what was happening. The ring looked like something that belonged on the finger of a movie star, not her, not June Harris.

"Will you marry me, June?"

She was speechless, her mouth agape with no sound coming out.

He exhaled. "I know I'm not what you hoped for. I'm not that college graduate. I'm not a good man. But I'll love you hard for the rest of my life."

"Yes," she managed to blurt out. June tugged his shirt to get him to his feet. "Yes."

Killian slipped the ring on her ring finger, and then kissed her on the mouth with so much passion her knees nearly gave out. "You're mine. And soon you'll be my bride."

She couldn't believe this was happening. How many nights had she dreamed of this? But it was real. Killian had come for her, and the hardcore bad boy was ready to love her for the rest of his life. It was surreal.

They rode into town on the Harley. Killian wanted to grab a quick bite to eat, and then he was going to drive her back to Bain and Scarlett's house for a couple days. She didn't want him to come back to help Killer of Kings because she was terrified something would happen to him, but he assured her the threat was gone, and it was only a matter of damage control. She could sacrifice a couple days for the sake of forever.

Once they parked in front of the coffee shop, a cruiser drove by and stopped beside them. It was Daniel, that jerk that wanted in her pants. She wondered if he suspected anything off about Killian. Her heart began to race as too many scenarios flashed in her head, many with Killian behind bars or worse.

"Where've you been? I've been looking all over for you," he said, coming around the front of his police car.

June frowned. "Why were you looking for me?"

"There's a lot craziness going on in town. Have you heard four different girls were kidnapped this week alone? A woman shouldn't be on her own these days."

Killian brushed her slightly behind him as he stepped forward. "She has me," said Killian, his voice carrying a distinct threat.

"For how long this time?"

He held her arm out to show Daniel her massive engagement ring. June was afraid to even guess how much it cost. "She said yes. That means I'll be taking care of her and *our* son. Always."

Daniel didn't even have the decency to congratulate them. He just shut up and got back in his car, driving away without a fight. Maybe he was smart. June couldn't imagine any man coming out on top of Killian. After a quick bite to eat, they swapped out the bike for his car and made the long drive out to Bain's home in the country. She was excited to see her son again, especially knowing she'd be able to give him the father he deserved.

"We're going to have a home, June. A real house, with a kitchen and garden and beautiful view of the ocean. I'm going to make it happen. Killian deserves everything I never had."

They held hands as they walked to the front door of the old farm house. Before they even knocked, Killian Junior bolted out the door and flung himself into her arms. She hugged him tight, and then kissed him on the cheek.

"Are we going home now?" he asked. June looked up at Killian, not sure what to tell her son just yet.

Killian bent down to Killian Junior's level and braced his shoulders. "I'm going to marry your mom, Killian. We're going to be a family. What do you think of that?"

He turned to June. "Is that true, Mom? You're going to marry him?"

"I love your father, Killian, always have. I want all of us to be happy together."

She saw the confusion on her son's face. It had always been the two of them, and he barely knew his dad. It would take some adjustment for all of them.

"Your mom's not going to be working at a damn bar anymore. She'll be there for you instead of killing herself working overtime. I'll take care of both of you. Things will be a lot different from now on."

"What if you leave us?"

Killian smiled. "Buddy, ain't going to happen," he said. "I love you, and no matter what you do, I'll still love you. Even if you hate me."

There was a moment of silence, the crickets droning all around them.

"We won't all fit in the bed."

June laughed. They shared a double bed in their tiny one-bedroom apartment back in town. She couldn't count the number of nights she'd quietly cried herself to sleep because she wanted better for them.

"We're not going back to the apartment, Killian. Your dad's going to buy us a house. A house by the water."

His eyes were wide with disbelief. "A house?"

Killian stood up and rubbed the top of their son's head, leaving his mop of blond hair a mess. "Of course a house. And your own bedroom. You like sports?"

"I play soccer at school."

"Perfect. I'll get nets for the yard, and we can practice together," said Killian

When she saw her son smile, genuine excitement lighting up his face, she couldn't stop the tears from welling up in her eyes. He deserved the very best. They'd been struggling for way too long.

"I'm going to tell Bain and Scarlett," he said as he ran into the house.

Once they were alone at the front of the house, Killian cupped the side of her face. "That's a good sign, eh?"

"Very good sign."

Killian kissed her, pulling her flush to his body. He grabbed her ass cheek, her dress bunching up in his hand. "Thank you for taking me back."

"Even though you were gone, I never stopped loving you," she said.

He nuzzled her neck, his hot breath sending shivers skittering along her skin. "You'll always be my girl," he whispered. "Love is just a word, so I'll spend the rest of my life showing you how much you mean to me."

The End

www.samcrescent.com

www.staceyespino.com

SAM CRESCENT & STACEY ESPINO

Killer of Kings

Taking Her Innocence
Broken Bastard

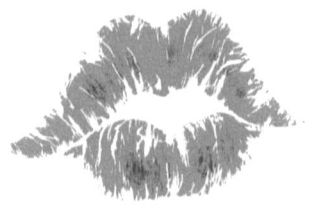

EVERNIGHT PUBLISHING ®

www.evernightpublishing.com